Praise for Janice Thompson's

BRIDAL MAYHEM MYSTERIES

"This series continues to be great! This book was just as wonderful as the others. The mixture, of suspense, humor, romance, and life in general is perfect. Then when you add in the inspirational thread it takes it over the top! Janice Thompson is an awesome author."

—WILANI WAHL, READER, REGARDING *CATERING TO DISASTER*

"I read a lot of different books. Some are so intense that I need a break from that type of book. Janice Thompson gives the reader a pleasant escape from life's challenges. This book is an easy read and a great escape to another place without it being so intense that it keeps you awake at night. It also teaches us not to jump to conclusions about people. Because things are not always what they appear to be."

—BARBARA GILL, READER, REGARDING *THE PERFECT MATCH*

"The groom goes missing two weeks before the wedding. Annie is on the case again trying to find what happened to him. A very good mystery and very funny book. Made me laugh out loud. Even her dog helps in finding Scott. More than a five star rating."

—JANICE SISEMORE, REGARDING *GONE WITH THE GROOM*

"Thompson's gentle sense of humor permeates this novel and ties into southern references including Annie's mother, who serves grits for breakfast every morning. This reader found herself laughing aloud more than once. A charming cast of characters is handled deftly by Thompson, who manages the whole passel with style and shows how a supportive family can band together in hard times. Between witty dialogue and fast action sequences, this novel kept my attention until the very (happy) end. *Gone with the Groom* is a great read for those who enjoy cozy whodunits with a bit of flair."

—LACY WILLIAMS

"Annie Peterson sets out to find out who stole a $25000 deposit from the bank depository. She hopes that in doing so, she'll clear her husband of the crime. From the moment Annie signs up for an online private investigator course until the satisfying conclusion of the book, Janice Hanna kept me thoroughly entertained. And maybe taught me a few lessons as well. The characters are delightful and so is the story. If you love a good cozy mystery, you won't be disappointed in *The Wedding Caper*."

—FRANCES DEVINE

"As a newly-inaugurated empty-nester, I could totally identify with the heroine of this story! A bank robbery; not one, but TWO weddings to plan; a host of suspects. SURELY it wasn't her husband. Or WAS it? A wonderful Christian read from one of my all-time favorite authors!!! Don't miss it!"

—REGINA MERRICK,
REGARDING *THE WEDDING CAPER*

DON'T ROCK THE BOAT

Bridal Mayhem Mysteries

Book 6

JANICE THOMPSON

Don't Rock the Boat
Copyright © 2016 by Janice Thompson.

All rights reserved. Except for use in any review, the reproduction or utilization of this work in whole or in part in any form by any electronic, mechanical, or other means, now known or hereafter invented, is forbidden without the permission of the author.

Printed in the United States of America.

Scripture taken from the HOLY BIBLE, NEW INTERNATIONAL VERSION®. Copyright 1973, 1978, 1984 Biblica. Used by permission of Zondervan. All rights reserved.

All of the characters and events in this book are fictitious. Any resemblance to actual persons, living or dead, or to actual events is purely coincidental.

More from JANICE THOMPSON

BRIDAL MAYHEM MYSTERIES SERIES

The Wedding Caper
Gone with the Groom
Pushing up Daisies
The Perfect Match
Catering to Disaster
Don't Rock the Boat

THE CLUB WED SERIES

Fools Rush In
Swinging on a Star
It Had to be You
That's Amore

THE BELLA NOVELLA SERIES

Once Upon a Moonlight Night
Tea for Two
Pennies from Heaven
That Lucky Old Sun
The Tender Trap

Dedication

In loving memory of Kay Malone, the real Sheila in my life. Our 2008 cruise was one of the highlights of my life. When I join you in heaven, we'll talk about how we lounged on a private beach in Cozumel, sailed aboard a pirate ship in Grand Cayman with swarthy seadogs, and swam in turquoise blue waters, so clear we could see our feet paddling below. I'll brag about how proud I was as I watched you climb Dunn's River Falls in Jamaica, and how tickled I got, every time you got turned around on the ship and led us in the opposite direction. More than anything, I'll laugh with you, just like we did on that seven-day adventure aboard the cruise ship. Until I see you on those heavenly shores (Get it...shores?), I will continue to live vicariously through Annie and Sheila, who are happy to sail on our behalf. I miss you, my dear friend, and can't wait to take the ultimate vacation with you, one that never ends.

Chapter One

ONLY THE OCEAN

God grant me a vacation to make bearable what I can't change, a friend to make it funny, and the wisdom to never get my knickers in a knot because it solves nothing and makes me walk funny.
—Anonymous

When you live in a landlocked state like Pennsylvania, the idea of taking a cruise on the open seas is both terrifying and mesmerizing. Terrifying, because you can't fathom the idea of seeing nothing but water for days on end, and mesmerizing, because stepping away from your mundane, landlocked life sounds over-the-top adventurous.

I've never been afraid of a little adventure, so, when my BFF, Sheila, suggested we go on an impromptu Caribbean cruise, I said yes. Actually, I said yes without even asking my husband, who, it turned out, wasn't quite as adventurous. Perhaps his life as a personal banker at the Clark County Savings and Loan was enough for him, but I wanted more, and I wanted it sooner, rather than later. Maybe, with a little persuasion, my hubby could be won over to my way of thinking. Surely he realized that my new status as an empty nest mom more than qualified me for a vacation. And what better early Christmas gift could the man give me, after all?

"Aw, c'mon, Warren." I paced our bedroom, nearly tripping over my two dachshunds, Sasha and Copper, who always seemed to be under foot. Sasha let out a little yip as I bumped her with the toe of my shoe. I gave her my most profuse apologies then turned back to my husband. "We'll only be gone a week, honey." I sat next to my hubby on the edge of the bed and gave him a pleading look. "You've got more vacation time than that, right? Don't they owe you two weeks?"

"Right." Tiny wrinkles formed in his brow as he raked his fingers through his messy salt and pepper hair. "It's not the time off I'm worried about, trust me. I could use a vacation. But it's just such short notice. Week after next?"

"We're getting the deal of a lifetime, from what the travel agent said," I argued. "Not a lot of people want to travel just before Christmas. You know?"

"I'm not sure, Annie." He put his hand on his stomach and gave me a thoughtful look.

"What? You get seasick?"

He paled a bit. "I don't know if I would or not. I've never been on a cruise before. The only boat I've ever been on is Orin's rowboat when we went fishing out on the river."

"And, as I recall, you had a wonderful time."

"I got sunburned and couldn't move for three days."

"Well, other than that, you had a terrific time, admit it."

"I lost four pounds because I couldn't keep anything down." He gave me a knowing look. "You remember how awful that was, right? The doctor said it was heat stroke."

"Well, sure, but the tummy issues were from the sun, not the boat, so there's hardly any comparison. Besides, they have those seasick patches now. People wear them on cruises all the time.

And trust me, the food is so good you'll forget all about being sick."

"How do you know the food is good? You're a cruising expert now?"

"No." I rose and paced the room. Sasha tagged along behind me, but Copper rested at Warren's feet. "I'm definitely not an expert. I only know what Sheila and Orin tell me. She said that the salt air will be the best thing for Orin, especially now that he's in remission." My eyes filled with tears as I thought about Orin's recent cancer treatment. I took a seat next to my husband once again. "Sheila's doing this for him, honey. And we're his friends. She wants us to come along for moral support."

"Might be hard to offer moral support if I'm in my cabin curled up in the fetal position."

"Honey, c'mon. We've been married a hundred and fifty years and you've never taken me on a cruise. We don't do anything adventurous."

"Annie." Warren gave me that I-can't-believe-you-just-said-that look. "We've been married thirty-four years."

"Thirty-three years this spring and we've never been on a cruise. Our honeymoon was a camping trip in the Ozarks."

"If I recall, we had a rollicking good time on that trip." A playful wink followed. "I don't remember any complaints."

Ah. So, this was the way to the man's heart. "We could have a rollicking good time on a cruise ship, too. Those little cabins are very romantic, from everything I've been told." I nudged up next to him and gave him a couple of sweet kisses. Before long, we were necking like teenagers.

When we decided to come up for air, Warren brushed back a loose hair from my face and smiled. "I'm just giving you a hard time, Annie. I already talked to Orin about the cruise this morning. He stopped in the bank to give me the particulars. I told him to count us in. I just wanted to string you along."

"You. . .you what?" I put my hands on my hips. "Do you mean to tell me I just stood here for ten minutes trying to convince you to do something that you've already done?"

"Fifteen minutes, but who's counting? And just for the record, we really have been married thirty-four wonderful years. Crazy, but wonderful years."

"We have?" I did the math in my head and then gasped. "Good gravy, we're getting old. We'd better take this cruise before I lose all ability to remember my own name."

A comforting smile followed from my sweet hubby as he gazed into my eyes. "Your name is Annie Peterson. You're married to Warren Peterson, the sexiest banker in the state of Pennsylvania." He gave me a passionate kiss, one that left little to the imagination.

"Alrighty then," I said when he released his hold on me. "You are definitely the sexiest banker in the state of Pennsylvania, and you happen to be married to the most amazing super sleuth in the town of Clarksborough and beyond."

"But not on the seven seas, right?" He gave me a pensive look. "Once we get out of Clarksborough, you'll put your sleuthing antennae down. Take a break?"

"Of course." I chuckled. "Trust me when I say that I have no desire to solve any crimes while we're on-board the cruise ship. My sole job will be to spend a little time resting and relaxing with you, Sheila and Orin. And eating. And going on excursions."

"Excursions?" His nose wrinkled. "You don't mean I'm going to have to go scuba diving, do you? I have inner ear issues, remember?"

"Good grief. No, I won't make you go scuba diving. But surely you wouldn't mind taking a couple of scenic tours, right? We're stopping in Cozumel first and I'm dying to do the private beach excursion. You can drink fruit punch from one of those coconut thingies while lounging on the beach. Sheila and I will snorkel."

"I'm trying to picture Sheila snorkeling." Warren paused a moment and then chuckled.

I had a hard time trying to picture it, too. To be honest, I'd rarely seen Sheila without her over-the-top makeup. No doubt she'd buy the waterproof version for our snorkeling adventure.

Not that I cared about such things. No, right now I only cared about one thing: picking out my new fun-in-the-sun wardrobe, boarding a flight to Texas, and hopping aboard the *Navigator of the Seas* in Galveston. Once I stepped onto that ship, nothing—and no one—could distract me. I'd settle back in my lounge chair and enjoy the ride. . .all the way to the Caribbean and back again.

Chapter Two

BEYOND THE SEA

Twenty years from now you will be more disappointed by the things that you didn't do than by the ones you did do. So throw off the bowlines. Sail away from the safe harbor. Catch the trade winds in your sails. Explore. Dream. Discover.
—Mark Twain

The two weeks leading up to the cruise passed like a whirlwind. Sheila and I made a couple of trips into Philly to shop for new cruising clothes, not an easy task during the winter season, and especially tough with so many Christmas shoppers pressing in around us. But we needed new bathing suits and we needed them now. Not that the idea of donning a bathing suit and prancing around in front of total strangers on a cruise ship held any appeal but Sheila insisted I'd get over that part in a hurry.

"Trust me, Annie," she said with a chuckle, "You'll see men and women in every shape and size and some of them are wearing two-pieces."

"Ugh." As long as I didn't have to see any grown men in

speedos, we'd be okay. Sheila couldn't guarantee that last part, though.

With no options available in the stores we eventually settled on a couple of skirted bathing suits that we found online. Thank goodness they arrived in time to land in our respective suitcases. I also purchased a lovely sundress, bright pink and yellow, just right for the tropics.

The night before we boarded our flight from Philly to Houston, I packed and re-packed my suitcase four times. At the last minute I contemplated adding a couple of things to the already bulging load. "Do you think I'll need a sweater?" I held up a brightly colored teal sweater in front of Warren.

He glanced up from the bills he was paying and shrugged. "It's the Caribbean, honey. It'll be hot, not cold."

"But it's cold here. And the plane will be cold. Don't you think?"

"Then wear a sweater on the plane."

"I will." A pause followed as I thought it through. "But sometimes it gets hot on planes."

Warren slapped himself on the forehead.

"Okay, okay," I said. "I'll wear a sweater on the plane and take another one for the cruise ship. It might get cold on-board. You know?"

"I *don't* know," Warren debated. "I've never been on one, and neither have you."

"Well, from what I've researched, it's cold."

Warren crossed his arms and gave me a knowing look. "Then why did you need my opinion on the sweater?"

Ugh! Such a man! "Because your opinion matters very much to me, Warren. That's why. And you always say I look good in sweaters."

He closed the checkbook and smiled. "Um, true. You do look good in sweaters. So, take it."

"I will." Gesturing to the suitcase, I said, "And I've got a couple more, too. And seven pairs of slacks, three pairs of jeans, six pairs of walking shorts, and more T-shirts and blouses than I can count. I sure hope my suitcase isn't over the weight limit on the plane."

"And I sure hope you're not going to quiz me on all of this later," my husband said. "Am I supposed to be taking notes?"

"Nah." I shrugged.

"Annie, we're only going to be on the ship seven days." Warren shook his head. "Why so much?"

"I just don't know what to expect and want to be ready for anything." I tried to close the suitcase and then zip it, but could not.

Warren sighed and then did it for me. "There. Now, please don't open it again. That's the fourth time I've closed it for you and it's getting harder every time."

"Oh, I have to open it again on the morning we leave. I'll have to put in my medications and my toothbrush and all that."

Warren slapped himself on the forehead once more and then reached over to grab his suitcase—his medium-sized, hardly full suitcase—and lifted it aright. "I'll put those things in my bag."

"Great idea. I'm glad you've got extra space because I'm sure I'll find some things to buy in Cozumel. And Cayman. And Jamaica."

"Just remember you'll have to pay customs fees if you buy too much." He gave me a knowing look.

"I know, I know." I sat on the edge of the bed, deep in thought. Sasha jumped up next to me and I scratched her behind the ears. "You gonna miss me, girl?"

Her tail wagged in response.

Copper sat at my feet and whimpered. I looked down at him and my eyes filled with tears. How could I leave my babies behind?

Don't Rock the Boat

"Do you think we could sneak these guys on-board?" I managed to ask above the lump in my throat. "Hmm? Two little stowaways? They would be a lot of fun."

"Are you kidding me?" Take these two mongrels on international waters?" Warren laughed. "If I know them, they'd jump overboard."

Heavens, no. "Not Copper," I argued. "He's scared of water. You saw what happened last time I bathed him."

"*You* bathed him?" Warren laughed. "That's priceless."

"Well, I *helped*. I brought you the towel. Point is, he's a scaredy-cat when it comes to water, so I doubt seriously he'll jump overboard."

"He's terrified of his own shadow," Warren reminded me. "No thank you. They'll do fine with Candy and we'll have a stress free time knowing they're in good hands."

"I guess."

"Besides, you'll be too busy eating and going on excursions to worry about the dogs. . . or anything else."

"Anything else?" I glanced his way and tried to figure out his meaning.

Warren's right eyebrow arched, quite the trick. "You. Know."

"I have no idea what you mean." I batted my eyelashes and feigned innocence.

"No crime solving on-board this ship, Annie Peterson." Warren crossed his arms at his chest. Was that a glare? How dare he!

"Can I help it if trouble seems to follow me everywhere I go?" I lifted my arms in mock despair. "I'm a crime magnet."

"You're a magnet, all right." He rose and slipped his arms around me. "And for the next week the only thing I want you gravitating to is me." He gave me a kiss that convinced me of that fact. I'd happily trade in my crime-fighting skills for another smooch like that. Maybe.

15

A couple of hours later, after dropping off the pups at Candy's place and grabbing a bite to eat at the local diner, Warren and I headed back home for what I hoped would be a good night's sleep. Instead, I tossed and turned all night.

Around three a.m. Warren grunted and then rolled over to face me. "Annie, with this much rocking and rolling, who needs a cruise ship?"

A sigh followed on my end. I really hadn't meant to disturb him. "I'm sorry, babe. I'm just so anxious. I haven't been on a plane in years, and what if you're right about getting seasick on the ship? I've only got a handful of those patches. Maybe we should stop at the drugstore on our way out and buy some Dramamine? And what if something goes wrong with Candy's pregnancy while we're gone? I mean, she could go into labor. You know? Then what?"

Warren groaned. "She's only seven months pregnant. I serious doubt she'll go into labor."

"What about Brandi? She's still in the first trimester of her pregnancy? She might need my help taking care of Maddy if she gets sick."

"She has a husband. He can help."

"Maybe Devin and Molly could help with Maddy if Brandi gets sick."

"Devin and Molly are still honeymooners. They need to be left alone." He yanked his pillow out from under him and then placed it over his face.

"True." I sucked in a couple of deep breaths. "What if Copper gets another pancreatitis attack?" I raised my voice in case Warren couldn't hear me from under the pillow. "He seems to go through that so much. I should've gone by the vet's office for more meds, just in case. And you know how Sasha is when we go away. She gets that separation anxiety thing. Candy won't know what to do. Ugh. This is impossible. What was I thinking?"

My husband rolled over, still clutching the pillow over his head. "Annie, take a sleeping pill." His muffled voice sounded from underneath. "I need some rest."

"It's too late for that," I argued. "It's three in the morning."

"Ten after three, and I'm going to be miserable in the morning." Warren tossed the pillow aside, got out of bed, walked into the bathroom and came back with a sleeping pill in one hand and a glass of water in the other. "Here. Take this so I can get some sleep."

"Okay, okay." I swallowed down the pill and then tossed and turned a few more minutes before drifting off. Crazy dreams followed. In one of them, Sheila and I were on a desert island, chasing a woman dressed as a bride. Nuts.

Warren woke me up at six-thirty, but I could barely remember my own name, what with the sleeping pill tugging my eyelids downward. I somehow managed to take a quick shower and dress, then climbed into the passenger seat of our SUV and leaned my throbbing head back against the headrest as Warren drove to Sheila and Orin's house. My BFF came bounding out of her front door just as we pulled into the driveway. As always, her wardrobe was a colorful ensemble that included bright teals and hot pinks. She definitely looked ready for a vacation in the tropics. If the clothing didn't convince me, the sun visor and sunglasses did.

Orin lugged two giant suitcases behind him and before long he and Warren had hefted them into the back of our vehicle. As Sheila climbed into the backseat, she talked a mile a minute about the upcoming cruise but all I heard was "Waa-waa-waa." The sleeping pill still threatened to lull me into a catatonic state.

"Cat got your tongue, Annie?" Sheila gave me a funny look.

"Uh-uh," I managed.

"She's drugged." Warren climbed into the driver's seat and reached for the key.

"Ooo." Sheila giggled. "Well, this oughta be a fun flight."

Frankly, I couldn't remember if it was a fun flight or not. I also couldn't remember if it was cold or hot on the plane. The minute we got on the 747, I leaned my head back against the seat, draped my sweater over my face and passed out cold. By the time I awoke, we were starting our descent into Houston. For the life of me, I couldn't figure out what we were doing in the air. It took a few minutes of 'coming to' for reality to settle in. Then, finally, excitement hit. We were going on a cruise! Yippee!

Minutes later, just as the lingering effects of the sleeping pill wore off, we were off of the plane and headed to the rental car area.

At this point, I really came alive. Suddenly, I could hardly wait to get to Galveston and to spend a few hours strolling on the beach with my honey. With the help of the GPS on my phone, Warren drove us from the airport in Houston to our hotel on the seawall. I'd heard about the Galvez hotel for years, and had seen it in pictures, but seeing the grand old hotel in person was pretty amazing.

We had a hard time making our way to the registration desk because of a large bridal party in line ahead of us. Turned out all of them—sixteen, in total—would be taking the same cruise. The wedding would take place in the chapel on the top deck of the ship on Tuesday evening at seven. All of this I learned from the bride-to-be, a girl named Meredith, who obviously felt comfortable sharing all of this personal information with me. She introduced her mother as Mrs. Williams—Betsy Williams—but I didn't get much out of her except a pained expression.

I empathized with this woman, of course. I'd already been the mother of the bride twice over and mother of the groom once. If time had allowed, I would've given her my years of wisdom in a heartfelt speech. Unfortunately—or fortunately, depending on how you looked at it—the wedding party got checked into the hotel, leaving us at the front of the line at the registration desk. I managed a "Maybe we'll see you on-board the ship" to Meredith then gave her a little wave as she walked off with the others.

"Isn't that sweet?" I sighed as I turned to face Sheila. "She's getting married in a couple of days."

"I don't envy her, having to pull off a wedding on a cruise ship, though." Sheila shrugged. "But that's their deal, not ours." She gave me a stern look. "Right, Annie?"

"Huh?"

"I know you. You're already thinking of ways to help them, aren't you?"

"Of course not." I paused. "Well, I did want to tell her that the photos should be done before the ceremony and it might also be helpful to know that the bride will be skittish on her big day, but that's nothing to be worried about. I mean, my girls were. Skittish, I mean. Then again, my girls were facing pretty big obstacles on their big days."

"And this bride is not. So, promise me you won't offer any suggestions, Annie." Sheila's gaze narrowed. "Promise?"

With the wave of a hand I dismissed the idea. "Seriously? I'll probably never see them again. Do you have any idea how many passengers there are on-board the *Navigator of the Seas*?"

"Yes. 3807. Approximately. Not counting crew, which adds another thousand or so." She slipped her arm through mine. "Now, let's mosey on up to our hotel rooms, slip on our bikinis and head to the beach while it's still sunny outside."

"Bikinis?" Orin sidled up next to her, room keys in hand.

Sheila gave him a little wink. "In your dreams, hot stuff."

Warren appeared next to me, dragging our luggage behind. "Did she say what I thought she said?"

I nodded. "Hey, where's the bellboy?"

Warren sighed. "I think they're all busy waiting on that wedding party. I don't mind dragging the bags to the room."

"I'll help." I reached for my suitcase and we headed off, ready to have the time of our lives.

Chapter Three

COME SAIL AWAY

You are now entering a stress free zone.

The rest of Saturday was spent walking the beach, not in bikinis, but in comfy shorts and t-shirts. The waters of the gulf weren't as pretty as I'd imagined—kind of a murky brown—but I had it on good authority—Sheila—that the Caribbean was a lovely shade of turquoise. We ate yummy seafood at Pleasure Pier, then headed back to the hotel. After a wonderful—okay, romantic—rendezvous with my hubby that night, I slept like a rock. In fact, I almost missed our wakeup call. I awoke with drool dribbling out of the corner of my mouth. Lovely.

Minutes later, we met with Orin and Sheila in the restaurant on the first floor, then pulled our bags to the lobby, where were waited alongside approximately a hundred other guests for the shuttle buses to arrive. Out of the corner of my eye I caught a glimpse of the mother of the bride-to-be. She looked a little... hmm. Pale? Maybe she wasn't feeling well.

Not that I paid much attention, of course. With the crowd pressing in around me, I could barely breathe. That same crowded feeling accompanied me on the bus, and during the registration process at the port. I'd never seen so many people crammed together like this before. Made my head swim. I actually felt a little nauseous. Where were those seasick patches, again? Oh yeah. . .loaded in my suitcase.

"You okay over there, Annie?" Warren asked. I could read the concern etched in the wrinkles between his eyes.

"Hmm? What?" I wiped some sweat off of my brow with the swipe of a hand. "Is it hot in here?"

"A little." He gave me a curious look. "I'm worried about you. You don't seem like yourself."

"Don't worry. Let's just get on that ship and I'll get some food. I'll be fine."

Turned out, getting on the ship took a little longer than I'd imagined. Passing off our luggage so that it could be taken to our cabin. Getting through customs. Having our photo taken for our Set Sail cards. Finalizing our expense accounts so that we could shop on-board. All of this took time. And just when I thought I'd finally made it through the worst of it, a photographer caught us and wanted to take a picture of our little group entering the ship. We somehow managed to get caught behind the wedding party. Again. Not that anyone was complaining. Well, anyone but Sheila, whose patience with this process was wearing thin.

By the time we arrived on-board the *Navigator*, however, all complaints were laid aside. All we could focus on was the luxurious Promenade deck and the over-abundance of gold and glass elevators. Wowza. I blinked, unable to take it all in.

"Where in the world are we?" Sheila shook her head as she looked around.

"This place is huge. Looks like a mall, only nicer." Orin's nose wrinkled.

"Much nicer," I agreed. I'd tried to envision what the *Navigator of the Seas* would look like in person, but nothing could have prepared me for the amazing space that stretched out in front of me with glamorous looking shops on either side. "Are you sure we're actually on-board the ship?" I looked around in an attempt to get my bearings. "Feels like a luxury hotel. And we're not rocking or anything like that."

"That's because we're still in port." Warren slipped his arm through mine. "I'm all for finding our rooms. We're on the 9th deck, right?" He glanced at his Set Sail pass and nodded. "Yep. Deck nine."

"Us too," Orin said.

Getting up to deck nine took some doing. Even with so many elevators in operation, we'd never make our way through the mob of people, so we took the stairs. Warren was huffing and puffing by the time we reached deck six. Orin looked like he might pass out by deck seven and I was practically crawling by deck eight. Only Sheila kept forging ahead, laughing and gabbing all the way. I guess her hours at the gym were paying off.

"C'mon, you wimps," she called out as we rounded the last turn on the stairway. "What's taking so long?"

None of us had the breath to respond. With the excessive pounding of my heartbeat in my ears, I couldn't think clearly anyway. Still, I finally put my feet on the floor of deck nine and breathed a sigh of relief. Finally. Home at last.

Well, almost home. Unfortunately, we turned the wrong way down a narrow hallway and lost our bearings. It took a little while, but we finally located our room: 932. Turned out, Sheila and Orin were in the room next to ours. We could thank our travel agent for that little blessing. Losing our friends on-board a ship this big would be catastrophic. Not that I could remember where we were. . .or how we'd gotten here. Were we forward or aft? Ugh. I didn't have a clue.

Our cabin, it turned out, was approximately the size of a postage stamp. Warren looked a little alarmed, especially when he saw the microscopic bathroom.

"Look on the bright side," I said. "You won't be spending much time in there, anyway."

"Unless I get seasick."

"Oh, that reminds me, Sheila told me we can buy more patches if we need them. They're in the shop on the deck two."

"We'll be fine." He walked over to the sliding glass door and opened it to step out onto the balcony. I followed behind him and shrugged when I saw that our only view, if one could call it that, was the port. I gaze down, down, down at the workers below, loading crate after crate of food products onto the ship.

"At least we won't go hungry." I offered Warren an encouraging smile.

"Is it dinnertime yet?" He glanced at his watch. "I'm starving. We missed lunch."

At that moment a knock sounded on our door. I answered to a giddy Sheila and Orin, who were in the mood to search the ship for food.

"Hey, did you see that the travel agent left us an onboard credit?" Sheila pointed to the small desk in front of the mirror. "Fifty dollars."

"Cool. What should we use it for?" I asked.

"Oh, a refillable soda bottle, maybe. Or a special meal in that fancy restaurant on the top deck. Or even Internet access. It costs a fortune to get on the Internet here, but fifty dollars would be a good start."

"Hopefully she won't need the Internet," Warren said. "Right, Annie?"

"Hey, I make no promises. I might decide to check in with the kids. You know?"

He sighed.

"Let's go up to the Windjammer Café on deck eleven," Sheila said. "They've got all sorts of yummy options, from what I read online."

We somehow made it through the crowd up to the 11th deck, where we joined approximately ten million other people in grazing on a variety of foods at the Windjammer buffet. Afterwards, the Captain got our attention on the loudspeaker, announcing a safety drill. Then, around five-fifteen Orin suggested we head back to our cabins to dress for dinner.

"Didn't we just eat?" Sheila asked.

"Well, sure." Orin gave her a curious look. "But I'm getting my money's worth and it starts today."

"So, is that what you plan to do to entertain yourself?" Sheila asked.

"I am," Orin said. "I'm gonna eat. And when I'm done with that, I'm going to sleep. And then I'm going to eat again."

"Well, I sure hope you'll go to the shows with us at night," I said. "It won't be the same if you don't. Warren will feel like the odd man out."

"With you and Sheila?" My husband laughed. "I'm always the odd man out."

"He has a point." Sheila grinned. "But don't you worry, folks. Orin's already promised me he'll do everything the rest of us do, shows and all."

"As long as she doesn't make me sing karaoke, we'll be just fine." Orin gave Sheila a little wink then pulled her into his arms for a kiss on the cheek.

"Mmm. I feel like bursting into song right now," Sheila said when he released his hold on her. She burst into an off-key rendition of *Some Enchanted Evening.*

It did turn out to be a pretty enchanted evening, just as Sheila had predicted. We showed up right on time for dinner and I let out a little whistle when I saw the luxurious three-story dining hall with the glittering chandelier in the center. "W-wow."

"Wow is right." Sheila's eyes practically bugged out of her

head. "This place beats anything I've ever seen."

"Fancy- schmaltzy," I added.

"But the men aren't dressed in suits like you said," Warren grumbled.

"Yeah, we're the only ones in suits and ties, Sheila," Orin loosened his tie a bit.

"No you're not," she argued. "Look around you. I see a lot of men dressed up nice and quite a few ladies in their Sunday best."

Orin rolled his eyes and I couldn't help but laugh.

The host seated us at a table—a large table, actually—near the center of the room. Turned out, we had assigned dinner guests: the bride and groom-to-be, along with another young woman and young man, who looked to be about the same age.

"Ooo, I remember you!" Sheila gave a little wave as she took her seat. "The bride and groom-to-be!"

"Yes, I'm Meredith." The gorgeous blonde bride gave us a warm smile from the opposite side of the table.

"And I'm Jake," the fiancé chimed in, his smile equally as contagious. "This is my best man, Kevin." He gestured to the guy nibbling on a piece of bread who glanced our way with a nod.

"And my maid of honor, Natalie." Meredith gestured to a young woman on her left who fidgeted with her napkin and then mumbled a quiet "Hello."

We did our best to engage the maid of honor as we ate our dinner, but she didn't seem terribly social. My gaze shifted to the best man, who greeted me with a welcoming smile. He reminded me of my son, Devin. My newly married son who rarely called his mama anymore. Tears sprang to my eyes at once.

Kevin turned out to be the life of the party, another thing he had in common with my Devin. He kept us entertained throughout the meal with stories about the bride and groom—especially the groom, who, it turned out, had a colorful past. Interesting. Still, we all found Kevin endearing.

Don't Rock the Boat

"Kevin's the reason we were able to take this cruise," Jake explained when the best man finally paused for breath. "His cousin Kenzie Jamison is one of the main performers in the 50s musical."

"And the other shows, too," Kevin explained. "She's a soloist. Studied at Julliard."

"Wow." Sheila gave him an admiring nod.

"She's also a great actress," Kevin added. "She did a show on Broadway last year. She's also a judge at the karaoke finals on Friday night, too."

"No joke?" I gave Kevin an admiring look. "Sounds like fun."

"You'll see her all over the ship. She performs on the top deck in the afternoons sometimes. She's in the Calypso band. She's always in some costume or another."

"Sounds like a great job."

"She loves it," Kevin said.

Jake nodded. "Thanks to Kenzie we all got a great price on the rooms. We really owe her."

Kevin puffed his shoulders in obvious pride. "She didn't mind. Just a gift for the bride and groom." His smile faded for a moment and then he shrugged. "I don't really get to see her much, anyway. She's always busy with rehearsals. But that's okay. My focus needs to be on my best friend." His gaze shifted—not to Jake, but to Meredith, who seemed oblivious. Interesting.

The bride lit into a conversation about her wedding gown, and kept all of us glued to her every word. Talk about a delightful young woman. Whatever concern I'd seen on her face back at the hotel was gone now.

Well, until her parents appeared at our table.

The mother of the bride approached with a pensive expression on her face. "I hate that we've been placed so far

27

away." She pursed her lips as she glanced back and forth between their two tables. "Doesn't seem fair." She gave me an imploring look. "Maybe we could switch places with you folks? Would you mind? I'd love to spend these next few days with my daughter." Her jaw clenched a bit. "Before she gets married, I mean."

"Oh, well, I wouldn't mind, but I don't know about the others." I glanced at Warren, who shrugged.

"Mama!" Meredith looked put off by her mother's suggestion. "It's fine. We have all day together. It won't hurt us one little bit to share our mealtime with people outside of the wedding party." She smiled at me. "In fact, let's just remedy that right now by inviting you to the wedding. What do you think? Tuesday night. Eight o'clock, in the chapel on the top deck. What do you say, Annie?"

"Well, I don't know. I. . ." My gaze shifted to her mother, who didn't look terribly happy that we'd been included.

"I'd love to have you there, Mrs. Peterson." Meredith reached for my hand and gave it a squeeze.

At this point, Meredith's mother huffed away. Jealous, perhaps? She had no reason to be, but how could I reassure her of that fact?

"I'm sorry about Mama," Meredith said. "I think it's the empty nest thing getting to her."

"I understand." And I did.

The bride's smile brightened. "Well, I still want you to come. The fact that you've been a mother of the bride so many times now convinces me we're going to get through this just fine."

"Well of course you'll get through it just fine." I offered what I hoped would be a convincing smile. "Just stay calm, cool and collected. And pray, honey. God's got this."

She nodded, but I saw a hint of disbelief in her eyes. Strange. Stranger still, the cool expression from the maid of honor. What in the world was up with that girl? If I had to judge from outward appearances, something I tried not to do, I'd have to guess she wasn't happy about the impending nuptials. In fact, as I caught her stealing a gaze at the groom-to-be, the strangest thought crossed my mind: Do you have the hots for your BFF's sweetie, perhaps? Hmm. Maybe.

I asked Sheila about it later as we strolled the top deck. Orin and Warren tagged along behind us, but were deeply engaged in conversation about our upcoming excursion to Cozumel.

"I picked up on it too." Sheila sighed. "It's a shame, you know? Those two girls are supposed to be best friends. Natalie should be happy for Meredith."

"Like you were happy for me when I solved that last case back in Clarksborough?"

"Well, sure." Sheila slipped her arm through mine just as a gust of wind threatened to topple us over onto the deck floor. "Whoa, there!" After calming down a bit she looked my way. "Just for the record, Annie, even if you didn't get it right every time I'd still stand by you. I don't love you because you jump through hoops."

I couldn't help but laugh at that one. "Well, that's good, because my hoop-jumping skills aren't what they used to be."

"I'm being serious." My friend's eyes filled with tears. "You've been the best friend I've ever had. I really mean that. You've been there for me, and for Orin, and I'm so grateful. This trip is just the icing on the cake."

I reached to give her a warm hug and whispered, "I agree."

Just then the fellas walked up behind us. "What's going on here?" Orin asked. "Some sort of a hug-in?"

"Yep, and you're invited." Sheila opened her arms and gestured for the guys to join us. Before long we were enmeshed in a group hug. Just about the time I felt emotions spill over me Warren muttered the word, "Awkward."

"Okay, okay." I released my hold. "But one of these days

you'll appreciate a warm hug from a friend, Warren Peterson."

"She's right you know." Orin sniffled theatrically, then threw his arms around my husband's neck. "You're the best friend I've ever had, Warren Peterson!"

"No, you're the best," Warren countered, volume rising.

"No, *you're* the best. I just *adore* you, Warren Peterson!" Orin's voice rang out, giddy and loud.

At that very moment an elderly couple happened by. "I've see this sort of thing on television, Bob," the woman said to her husband as she gave Warren and Orin a curious look, "but never in person. My goodness."

My husband released his hold on Orin in a hurry and before long we were all laughing so hard we could barely contain ourselves.

"C'mon, Annie," Warren said. "Let's go back to the cabin. I'm starting to feel woozy."

I was starting to feel woozy, myself. Might have a little something to do with seasickness, or it might have more to do with the odd scene now going on to my right. Was that the infamous maid of honor standing in the moonlight with the groom-to-be? Before I could tell for sure, they both disappeared through the doors into the interior of the ship. Very, very odd.

Not that it was any of my business, of course. Still, as a former mother-of-the-bride, I had to keep an eye on things... didn't I? Well, of course I did!

Chapter Four

SEA OF LOVE

The alternative to a vacation is to stay home and tip every third person you see.
—Author Unknown

Our first full day at sea was crammed full of on-board adventures. We ate breakfast at the Windjammer Café at 8:30 a.m., played music trivia in the lounge on deck four at 10:00 a.m., watched a Bingo game in the theater at 11:15, ate lunch on the top deck by the pool at noon, played cards in the library at 1:30 p.m., napped from 2:00 to 4:00 and sat out on our balcony watching the waters beneath the ship as the colors changed to the most majestic shade of deep blue I'd ever seen.

Around four-thirty we headed up to the top deck. Off in the distance the band played a reggae tune, something with a lot of action and pizazz. I couldn't help but notice the singer, a gorgeous girl with jet-black hair and tanned skin. She looked like a cover model. Well, except for the over-the-top calypso outfit she wore. That looked a little more like Carmen Miranda. I turned my attention to the belly flop competition. I had no idea what to expect, but apparently it involved several highly intoxicated overweight men seeing who could create the biggest splash in the pool. Ugh. Not my cup of tea.

Speaking of tea, I needed something to drink, so left hubby and friends to refill my soda bottle with my favorite diet drink. Seated at a nearby bar with a soda in hand, I found the best man. He smiled as I approached.

"Mrs. Peterson."

"Kevin, isn't it?"

"Yes."

"What? You weren't in the belly flop contest?" I teased as I handed my drink bottle to the bartender and gave him my order.

"Um, no." Kevin rubbed his stomach. "Though, if I keep eating like this I'll be more than qualified." The laughter that followed caught the attention of a man to his left who rolled his eyes.

"Hardly," I said. "So, are you alone? Where's the rest of the bridal party?"

"They're in the hot tub. Or the pool. Not sure. I wanted to sneak away to hear Kenzie sing."

"Kenzie?"

"My cousin. She's a singer." He gestured to the young woman in the band, the one with the Carmen Miranda dress."

"Oh, wow. She's your cousin?"

"Yes. She was also in the show last night. Did you see it?"

"We did. No wonder she looks familiar. Very talented girl."

Kevin laughed. "Yeah, well. . .she's the only one in the family who got the talent, trust me. I'm an accountant, not a singer or actor."

"You're an accountant?" That really piqued my interest. "Then you'll have a lot in common with my husband. He's a banker." This led to a lengthy chat about investment portfolios, which apparently bored the guy sitting next to Kevin. When he left, I took his seat and we kept talking…until Warren showed up.

"Annie?" My husband gave me a curious look. No doubt. He'd never seen his wife bellied up to a bar before. "We thought we lost you."

"Sorry." I laughed. "Got to talking. Did you know Kevin here is an accountant?"

Well, that was all she wrote. Warren ended up taking my seat at the bar and after a minute or two I'd lost him to the conversation with Kevin. I turned my attention back to Kenzie and the band. They wrapped up their set and she headed our way. As she drew near, I noticed the most unusual tattoo on her upper right arm. Angel wings. Beautifully done.

Kevin made introductions. Before long we were all laughing and talking. Kenzie couldn't stay long because she had a rehearsal in the theater, but I gushed over her acting and singing abilities before she left.

"Wow." I turned back to Kevin and gave him an admiring smile. "She's great."

"I know. She had a lot of training. Graduated from Julliard."

"Oh, I agree her singing is great, but I just meant as a person. She seems really sweet."

Kevin rose from the bar stool and stretched. "Well, what do you expect? She's originally from Texas. We're all friendly in Texas, you know."

This got a chuckle out of all of us. Kevin said his goodbyes and headed off to find the others at the pool.

Warren grabbed my bottle and took a sip of my diet drink, then wrinkled his nose. "Ugh."

"I know, I know. But I like it. And besides, I've got to watch my girlish figure."

"*I'll* watch your girlish figure." He gave me a little wink. "Just let me do it with a real soda in hand."

"Okay, okay." I passed the bottle back to the bartender and exchanged the diet soda for a 'real' one.

Warren took a big sip. "Ah, that's more like it." He shifted his attention to the now-empty stage where the Calypso band had been.

Just then, Sheila and Orin appeared, plates in hand.

"You should taste this cheesecake, Annie," Sheila said. "It's delish."

"Aren't we going to dinner in an hour?" I asked. My gaze shifted to the yummy looking cheesecake on her plate.

"Well, yes, but this is just an appetizer." She poked her fork in the cheesecake and then passed it my way. "Here, try this."

I did. And then I took another bite. And another. Best appetizer ever.

"If you think that was good, you should've seen the pastries. Who serves pastries in the middle of the day? The *Navigator of the Seas*, that's who!" She laughed and took her fork back.

"What are you guys doing out here?" Orin asked.

"Listening to the band." I gestured to the stage. "We were, anyway. They just ended their set."

"Ah. Did we miss much?" Sheila tossed her plate in a trashcan and then leaned against the bar.

"Actually, yes. Kevin was here. We had a long talk."

"Kevin?" Creases formed in-between Orin's eyes.

"The best man," Sheila said. "Remember? We met him last night."

"Oh, right." Orin shrugged. "I wasn't taking notes."

"Remember he told us his cousin works on-board the ship?" I said. "Well, I just met her. She was the singer in the Calypso band and she was that gal who impressed us all so much in the show last night."

"Oh, wow." Sheila looked impressed by this news. "I remember her. Talented gal."

"Very." I nodded. "We met her in person just now. Sorry you missed her. She seems like a real sweetie, just like Kevin."

"Nice guy," Warren added. "An accountant."

"Well, that explains why you like him." Sheila gave Warren a nudge with her elbow. "But what's your fascination, Annie?"

My eyes welled with tears. "He just reminds me so much of Devin. I mean, his hair color is different. And his eyes aren't the same shade. And he's a lot taller and thinner than Devin, but other than that. . ."

"Annie, they have nothing in common." Sheila rolled her eyes.

"Well, of course they do," I argued. "They're both sweet young men."

"I'd be willing to bet he's sweet on Meredith."

I couldn't help but gasp. "You noticed it, too?"

"C'mon, Annie. I might be old, but I'm not blind. I have eyes in my head. I saw how he was looking at her last night."

"Yeah." I sighed. "I noticed it, too." Of course, I'd also noticed the groom-to-be hanging out in the moonlight with the maid of honor, but I didn't bother to mention that.

"Don't you two have anything else to talk about?" Warren shook his head.

"Yeah, like dinner?" Orin added. "I'm hungry."

We all turned to stare at him.

He rubbed his stomach. "What?"

"Oh, nothing." I laughed. "I guess it is time to head back to our cabins to dress for dinner."

I led the way across the deck to the elevators. Off in the distance I caught a glimpse of the bridal party getting out of the hot tub. The groom seemed in a great mood but the maid of honor still looked a bit sullen. I'd love to know her story.

"Annie?" Warren nudged me and I startled to attention.

"Hmm?"

"Stay focused, girl. You almost walked into a pole."

"Oh?"

"Eyes on the road, Annie." Sheila laughed. "We want to make it to dinner in one piece."

Less than an hour later, after returning to our cabins and dressing for the evening, we did make it to dinner in one piece. Well, unless you counted the part where Sheila's slip was hanging out from the back of her skirt. She fixed it right there in the dining room with everyone looking surrounding us, but no one seemed to notice.

Except the mother-of-the-bride, who stood watch over our table like a queen over her subjects. She gave Sheila a 'You're so inappropriate' look and then walked over to her own table.

"Don't mind my mama," Meredith said and then sighed. "She's a little out of sorts."

She seemed a l-o-t out of sorts to me, but I didn't say so. Instead, I took my seat, ordered the finest meal on the menu, and stuffed myself silly. With the bridal party in good spirits, we had a lovely evening, all the way down to dessert, where I ordered the key lime pie.

Afterwards we went to the theater to watch the musical extravaganza and I marveled as I watched Kenzie in action one more time. Man, could that girl sing, or what? She amazed me with her talent. And all of these old songs made me want to sing along. So, I did. I sang every single one. In the seat to my right, Sheila sang along, too. In fact, she sang so loudly at one point that Orin jabbed her with his elbow. That didn't accomplish anything. She just kept singing. And singing. And singing.

Even with her off-key voice ringing out beside me, I found the whole evening enjoyable. In fact, I didn't have one complaint about the past several hours. What a blissful day at sea it had been.

We talked about it at length as we nibbled on cookies at the café on the Promenade Deck. We laughed and talked about how we all wanted our children to send us on cruises instead of putting us in retirement homes. After a lot of yawning on Orin's part, I knew the time had come to head back to our rooms. We made our way through the crowd, up the elevators to the 9th floor. I noticed the maid of honor standing alone in the corner of the elevator and tried to greet her, but she turned the other way. So strange.

I thought about it all the way to our cabin. Was the girl just anti-social or was there something more going on? I couldn't tell, but the sadness on her face did make me think that she needed my prayers, at the very least. I'd have a long talk with the Almighty about her. Surely He would clue me in.

Once we said our goodnights to Sheila and Orin, I headed inside the cabin on Warren's heels. We discovered the stateroom attendant had morphed one of the towels into a monkey-like creature. It hung from a coat hanger above our mirror. When I first saw the reflection of the little guy in the mirror I jumped.

"Ooo, that startled me."

"That stateroom attendant is one talented guy." Warren walked over to the monkey and touched it.

"I do not possess the towel-morphing talent." Even as I spoke the words, I was reminded of what Kevin had said about Kenzie. She was the one in the family who'd gotten all of the talent. I guess some people just had more of it than others. For now, though, the only talent I possessed was the 'let's-see-who-can-get-into-their-PJs-the-quickest-and-fall-asleep-on-board-the-Navigator-of-the-Seas."

Turned out, I was pretty good at snoozing aboard the high seas.

Chapter Five

WATER YOU WAITING FOR?

We hit the sunny beaches where we occupy ourselves keeping the sun off our skin, the saltwater off our bodies, and the sand out of our belongings.
—Erma Bombeck

I awoke Tuesday morning to the sound of the captain's voice, announcing we were docked in Cozumel. I didn't even bother putting on a robe. I pulled open the glass sliding door to the balcony and raced outside for a peek. Turned out we were on the ocean side, not the dockside. Still, I could see a bit of land in the distance.

After dressing for the day and enjoying a quick breakfast in the Windjammer we made our way through the crowd, past security, and off of the ship. I'd waited for this moment for days and my heart could barely contain my joy and excitement.

The gorgeous waters at the pier took my breath away. Quite a difference from what I'd seen in Galveston. Such an exquisite tealish-blue. Wow. "Oh, Warren, look!"

"I would," he responded, "but I can't seem to get my land legs."

Indeed. He did look a little wobbly.

With Sheila leading the way—nothing unusual there—we headed off to find our tour guide for the private beach excursion. Five minutes later we were standing in line with approximately 200 other tourists. Five buses lined the edge of the road, all with different numbers.

"Did you remember the sunscreen?" Sheila asked.

I nodded. "You betcha. We're pretty close to the equator here, right? I'd fry like a fish without my sunscreen."

"Yep. Not that I'd mind a tan. I'm as white as a sheet. Except my age spots." She stuck out her arm to show me a spot so small I could barely find it.

"Sheila, that's a freckle."

"No, it's an age spot. It wasn't there two weeks ago. Now it is."

I leaned down and gave it a closer look. "Are you sure it's not a freckle?"

Sheila just sighed then looked away. Moments later, she turned back to face me. "Oh Annie, look! The wedding party!" She pointed at our dinner guests and began that frantic waving thing Sheila was so famous for. Before long the bride waved back. The groom didn't seem to notice us, but the bride's mother did. She gave us a curt nod and turned back to her family.

"Not very friendly, is she?" I asked.

"Well, you know how it is, being the mother of the bride, Annie." Sheila gave me a scolding look. "Her daughter's getting married tonight, after all. Maybe she's stressed."

"Well, if she's stressed, she's the only one in the wedding party who is. I've never seen a bride-to-be so laid back." A chuckle followed as I watched the gorgeous young blonde laugh with her friends.

At our tour guide's instruction we boarded bus #22. The bride and groom were on our bus, as was the best man, but the rest of their bridal party was divided amongst the other buses. This, according to Meredith, who seemed very chatty.

"It's my wedding day!" she squealed. "Only ten hours left until I'm Mrs. Jake Kennedy." Her eyes brimmed with tears and she leaned her head on her groom's shoulder. The words "I can't wait" came out as a whisper.

They looked so sweet sitting there I almost cried, myself.

Instead, the bus driver drew my attention out of the window as the vehicle jolted and then took off down the crowded city street. We followed behind the other buses all the way through town then made a turn on a narrow tree-lined drive. I'd never seen so many palm trees in my life. Everything was so green and lush.

"I could live here." A contented sigh followed as I thought it through. "Sasha and Copper would love it."

"And the kids? Would we bring them, too?" Warren asked.

"Of course. Couldn't survive without them. We'll build a huge mansion on the water, big enough for everyone."

"And who's funding this mansion?" my husband asked.

"You are." I turned to face him. "You can become an international banker."

At this proclamation, Warren rolled his eyes.

We didn't have time to discuss it further because Sheila went off on a tangent about tropical fruits she wanted to eat on the island. Orin chimed in, reminding us that the beach had an all-inclusive buffet. Not that I felt like eating. No sir. I just wanted to dip my toes in the warm waters of the Caribbean.

Minutes later, I did just that. While Sheila and Orin nabbed four lounge chairs and a couple of umbrellas, I headed out to the water's edge and marveled at God's handiwork. I could hardly contain my joy. Seconds later, my husband joined me.

"Couldn't wait, could you?"

I shook my head. "Oh, Warren." My eyes filled with tears as I took in the white sand beach and rippling turquoise water. "Have you ever seen anything so beautiful?"

He shook his head. "No, but it's making my stomach churn. Do you think we could get the beach to stop moving?"

"The beach isn't moving, honey...only the water. You want to dip your toes in?"

"I think I'd be better off in a lounge chair with a bottle of water." His brow wrinkled. "Do you think it's safe to drink the water here?"

"Yes, didn't you hear the announcement from the tour guide? It's bottled water."

"Yes, bottled, but where does it come from?" For a minute, Warren looked like he might be sick. He clammed his eyes shut and I was pretty sure I could see him mentally counting to ten.

"Nauseous?" I asked.

"Mm-hmm. Maybe I'd better put a patch on, after all." He made his way to a lounge chair and plopped down. Orin took the seat to his left.

I dropped my beach bag onto the chair to Warren's right and turned back to talk to Sheila. She had somehow already peeled off her cover-up and was prancing down to the water's edge in her skirted one-piece.

"Hey, wait for me!" I scrambled out of my cover up and jogged over to meet her, jogged being a loose term, since I was still so full from our massive breakfast. I found her with tears flowing as she gazed out across the water.

"Oh, Annie, isn't God good?"

"He is."

For a moment neither of us said a word. Then, just as quickly the holiness of the moment was shattered by the sound of a little boy's voice as he kicked sand on our legs.

"John Paul, you tell those ladies you're sorry!" His mother's voice rang out from behind him.

The impish youngster looked at us and giggled. "Sorry! I was just having fun!"

"You're forgiven." Sheila knelt down beside her. "Don't forget to put on sunscreen, okay?"

"Mama already put it on." His little nose wrinkled. "It's sticky."

"Maybe, but it's for your own good. You don't want to get sunburned."

"Oh, that reminds me," I said as the boy and his mother headed off down the beach. "We'd better put on sunscreen too, Sheila." I made my way back to the lounge chairs, where I found Warren moaning and groaning. He pulled a towel over his head and begged the clouds to stop moving. Yikes. I reached for my bag and came out with the sunscreen. At least, I thought it was sunscreen.

"Oh no."

"What's wrong, Annie?" Warren's gravelly voice sounded from underneath the blanket.

"This isn't sunscreen at all. It's suntan oil. For deep, dark tan. Ugh."

"Well, that's what you want, right? A deep, dark tan?"

"Absolutely not. I want a light golden bronze, with no hint of red."

"Good grief." Warren rolled over and I could tell I'd lost him. At least he stood no chance of being burned, curled up like a burrito under that towel.

Sheila appeared at my side a moment later. "Can I borrow your sunscreen?"

"I wish." A groan followed on my end. "It's not really sunscreen at all." I explained the situation to her and she shrugged. "Oh well. Let's get a deep, dark tan, Annie. We only live once."

"Yeah, I only lived once, and I'd like to go on living, thank you very much."

A couple of minutes later, lathered in oil, we pranced like kids to the water's edge, then eased our way in. I'd expected it to be warm, but chilly might've been a better description. It was December, after all.

Sheila and I finally made it in to our waists. Then, moments later, we garnered the courage to stick our heads under. After that, we really got brave. Sheila ran back to shore and grabbed our snorkeling gear. We spent the next several minutes searching for fish and coral.

We didn't locate any of the colorful coral I'd hoped for, but did see lots and lots of fish. They took my breath away. Okay, maybe the clogged breathing apparatus took my breath away. I shook it out and sucked in a couple of deep breaths of fresh air. The sting of salt water in my eyes blurred my vision, so I rubbed and rubbed until I could see clearly. Off in the distance I noticed the bride and groom-to-be in the water. Kissing. I bit back the temptation to holler, "Get a room." They were getting married tonight, after all. They eventually made their way back to shore. Sheila, probably a bit waterlogged, decided we should do the same. Oh, but I didn't want to get out of the water.

"I could live here," I said as I flipped to my back to float a while.

"Go ahead," she said. "But if you want me, I'll be up on the lounge chair, soaking in the sun."

"Okay, okay." I made my way out of the water and slogged my way through the deep sand to the lounge chairs. I found Warren covered head to toe with a huge towel. I nudged him awake and we all headed to the all-you-can-eat buffet, where we chowed down on fish—lots and lots of fish. And fruit. And rice. And black beans. And tortillas. And more fish. And two desserts. Okay, three desserts. Afterwards, bellies full, we headed back to our lounge chairs.

At this point I noticed one of the workers moving up and down the beach selling his wares. Fruit punch in those little coconuts, it looked like. Something about the way he acted when he approached the bridal party made me nervous, and all the more as Meredith toweled off nearby. The guy didn't take his eyes off of her. Then again, she was a pretty young thing, especially in that hot pink two-piece. Any guy with eyes in his head would notice. I did my best to lay any suspicions aside.

I sat in the lounge chair next to Warren and tapped his leg. He startled to attention and pulled the towel off of his face. "Hmm? Annie?"

"Did you guys happen to notice that guy on the beach?" I gestured to the man, who still stared at the bride "The one selling drinks?"

"Eduardo?" Orin nodded. "He seemed pretty nice. I bought some water from him. He assured me it was safe."

"Yeah, well, something about him is bugging me," I said. "He can't take his eyes off of Meredith."

"She's wearing a bikini, Annie." Sheila gave me a knowing look. "You know?"

"Right. I wish he'd put his eyes back in his head, though."

"Very few men put their eyes back in their head with a pretty girl around." Warren gave me a wink and then pulled the towel back over his head.

I settled back into the lounge chair and tried to put Eduardo out of my mind. Before long, I was snoozing in the sun. When I awoke, I had the weirdest sensation on my face. It stung. Bad. So did my arms, for that matter.

Seconds later the announcement came over the loudspeaker for us to leave, and Warren came out from under his towel. He took one look at me, rubbed his eyes as if not quite believing what he saw and then said, "Um...Annie?"

"What?"

"You're. . .you're a lobster."

"I'm what?" Still trying to come fully awake I glanced down at my legs. They were as red as the logo on the umbrella above. No way. So much for a dark golden tan.

I looked at Sheila, who still snoozed in the chair to my right. Oh. My. Goodness.

I'd never seen that color on a human before. She was sort of an orangey-red. Very, very odd. I tried calling her name but she didn't respond. I poked her in the side and she came bounding up. At once she hollered, "Ouch, ouch, ouch!" and pointed to her face. Then her arms. Then her legs.

"Yeah, me too." I tried to stand, but couldn't. My knees didn't want to bend. Warren helped me. Sheila managed to stand, too—with Orin's assistance—but I could see the pain etched in her face. I felt it, too.

We made our way back to the buses, passing several shops along the way. I caught a glimpse of the bride in one of the shops, fruit punch in one hand and pocketbook in the other, and gave her a nod. Her eyes widened when she saw me.

"I know, I know." With the wave of a hand I tried to dismiss any concerns she might have. The girl was getting married in a few hours. She didn't need to be worried about little old me.

I was worried about little old me, though. And my worries grew more exaggerated when I tried to board the bus. My knees, now swollen, didn't want to bend. The bus driver clucked his tongue as he helped me and muttered "Sunscreen."

"I know, I know." I groaned as I made my way to the top step. "I wanted a dark, golden tan."

"It's dark, all right." Warren voice sounded from behind me. "But I wouldn't call it golden."

"Very funny." I wanted to stick my tongue out at him, but right now I had other things to do. . .like getting to my seat.

I somehow managed. Once I settled down, Warren took the

spot next to me. Sheila and Orin sat behind us—a real problem, since Sheila went on and on and on about her pain level. All of this chatter about pain certainly wasn't helping mine any.

The groom-to-be tossed his bag into the seat in front of us and looked my way, his brow knotted. "Mrs. Peterson..."

"Call me Annie." I tried to shift my position but could not. My burnt thighs wouldn't allow it.

Jake glanced at his watch, then back at me. "Annie, we're looking everywhere for Meredith."

"Meredith? What do you mean?"

"She's missing. We haven't seen her since we left the beach."

I tried to wave my hand to dismiss his concerns but my arm was stiff from the sunburn. "Oh, not to worry," I said. "I just saw her in one of the shops. Maybe she's buying you a little wedding gift." I tried to give him a wink but my now-swollen eyelid wouldn't cooperate.

"Are you sure?" Jake didn't look convinced.

"Yep. She was in the jewelry store."

"I'll go check."

"Better hurry," Warren said. "We're about to leave."

"I will." Jake took off in a flash. I tried to close my eyes, but they felt so strange. From behind me, Sheila went on and on about her pain level, which completely aggravated mine.

"Do you have to do that, Sheila?" I did my best to turn to face her, but she looked kind of fuzzy. Then again, everything looked fuzzy. And my stomach felt really squishy all of a sudden.

A couple of minutes later Jake was back with Kevin at his side.

"She's not here?" He looked around, as if he'd expected her to magically appear in his absence.

I shook my head. Well, I tried to, anyway. "No. She wasn't in the shop? I was sure I saw her there."

"No." Kevin shook his head. "We looked there. Just an older

woman at the cash register and that guy who was selling water on the beach. No one else."

"The guy with the water on the beach?" Hmm.

The bus driver climbed aboard and closed the door. His voice came over the loudspeaker, welcoming us back. Seconds later we were pulling away from the beach. There would be no looking for Meredith now. I tried to keep my heart calm, but a sense of dread came over me. I did my best not to let it show.

Kevin took a seat but Jake stood in the aisle until the bus driver asked him to sit down. Then he eased his way down into his seat, a look of confusion still registered on his face. "I didn't think to bring my cell phone."

"I've got mine." Sheila whipped it out. "What's her number?"

Jake gave her the number and we waited. And waited.

Sheila shrugged and said, "Voicemail."

"Where's everyone else in the bridal party?" Warren asked. "In the other buses, right?"

"Right."

"Maybe she's with the maid of honor?" I tried.

I could see the relief on Jake's face the moment I mentioned this possibility. "Good point. They're all spread out on other buses. I'm sure that's what happened. She's with Natalie. Or her mom. Or someone else." He nodded. "We'll laugh about this later, I'm sure. Just kind of freaked me out that we're headed back to the ship and she's not with me. She's always with me."

"And she'll always be with you." I gave him an encouraging smile. "I can tell that girl adores you."

"She's the best thing that's ever happened to me. I'm the luckiest man alive."

"Blessed," I countered. "You're very, very blessed."

He nodded. "Yes. Very."

"Don't worry about Meredith," I said. "Trust me when I say that a bride usually doesn't see her husband-to-be on the day of the wedding so she's probably holding to that tradition in these final hours."

"Trust me, there's been nothing traditional about this wedding." He shrugged. "We wanted it that way, but her mother... " His words trailed off. "Anyway, her mom usually wins out. Meredith and I wanted to get married in our home church, back in Texas, but she thought this would be more fun."

"It will be fun," I said. "You'll make memories no one will ever forget."

"Right."

At this point Sheila engaged him in a conversation about the upcoming wedding and he reminded us that we were all invited. "Just after dinner," he said. "So come dressed and ready."

I nodded, but I couldn't imagine getting dressed with this sunburn being so bad. Right now all I wanted to do was dive into a cold swimming pool and pray this pain would subside. Hopefully, once I got back on the ship, I could do just that.

Chapter Six

BRIDGE OVER TROUBLED WATER

I don't know who named them swells. There's nothing swell about them. They should have named them awfuls.
—Hugo Vihlen

When we arrived at the pier, Jake took off to search for his bride-to-be. We would've joined him, but, frankly, couldn't keep up. In fact, I could barely stand up. Sheila, who'd fallen asleep in the bus, was in even worse shape when we woke her. She actually cried. Real tears. If I looked anything like she did, we'd be the reddest guests at the wedding tonight.

If we made it. Right now, just getting off the bus took forever. And once we managed that—Lord help us—getting back to the ship would also be a challenge. I could barely move without wanting to weep.

Somehow we made it. I got through customs, boarded the *Navigator of the Seas*, and then went straight to the pool on the top deck. The guys went back to the cabins, Sheila joined me in the pool. We settled into the cold water and the sunburn instantly felt better.

"Ahhh." She smiled for the first time all afternoon and then released an exaggerated sigh. "I might just live after all."

"Me too." Just about that time an elderly woman got into the pool with us. She took one look at the two of us and gasped. "For pity's sake." She turned to the man getting into the water behind her. "Earl, would you look at this? These poor ladies." She clucked her tongue and went on and on in motherly fashion, giving us all sorts of advice about how to deal with the pain.

"Do you have any Aloe Vera?" she asked.

I nodded. "In the room. Brought it just in case."

"Well, you two need to take out stock in some," she said. "Because you look bad."

"Really, really bad." Her husband said, his eyes wide.

Gee, thanks a lot.

We stayed in the pool until four-thirty then climbed out to head to the room. Something about the hot sunshine on my cold wet body caused a weird stinging sensation. If we made it to dinner and the wedding it would take a miracle. Right now I just wanted to live in the swimming pool.

"Promise you'll put on Aloe the minute you get to your room!" the elderly woman called out.

I nodded then took off for my cabin with Sheila on my heels, complaining the whole way. In the elevator we happened to see Kenzie, dressed in beach attire.

She gave us an incredulous look and shook her head, her mouth rounding into a perfect "O." "Wow, you two look. . ."

"I know, I know." I groaned. "Burnt."

"I always use sunscreen." She offered us a smile. "Learned the hard way."

"Were you at the beach too?" Sheila asked. "Figured you'd have rehearsal or something."

Don't Rock the Boat

"They give us a break when we're in port. Sometimes, anyway." She smiled and then exited the elevator on the 10th floor. We went on down to the 9th and got off, then somehow made it to our cabins.

With Warren's help I got out of my swimsuit and into the shower. I cried the whole time. Afterwards, I decided to air dry. Touching a towel to my skin seemed impossible, at best. Still, the tears flowed. Warren helped me put on the Aloe, gently applying it to all of the places I could not reach. It felt cool to the skin, which helped, at least for a moment. Then, just as quickly, it felt like a seal on my skin, which now felt like it was cooking. The tears came again.

Warren gave me a sympathetic look. "Annie, I've been with you through the birth of three children and don't think I've ever seen you this worked up."

"I. . .I know." The tears flowed, which only aggravated things because they were hot against my burnt cheeks. "This is mi... miserable!" I eased my way down onto the bed—completely naked—and sent Warren off to deliver the Aloe to Sheila's cabin. When he came back his eyes were huge.

"Wow. Just. . .wow."

"What?" I asked.

"She never made it out of her bathing suit. I seriously doubt we're going to dinner tonight."

"We're going, all right." I tried to stand. "I'm going to wear my sundress, but we're going, by golly. And we're going to the wedding too. It's at eight o'clock and I promised Meredith and Jake we would be there."

"Don't you think, under the circumstances, they would forgive us?"

"Yes, but I'm not one to go back on my word."

And so, with teeth gritted, I somehow got into my underclothes and my sundress. I couldn't stand the feel of my bra straps on my burnt shoulders, so I pulled them off and tucked them under my arms. "There you go," I said. "A do-it-yourself-strapless-bra."

Warren just shrugged. "Well, I'd say it's sexy but this might not be the right time."

"Trust me, there's nothing sexy about how I feel right now." I walked over to the mirror to put on makeup, took one look at my red-orange face and gasped. "Holy cow. Well, I guess I don't need blush." I did swipe on a bit of lipstick and reached for the mascara wand. "Okay. I'm ready."

"What about Sheila and Orin?"

I turned away from the mirror. "If I know Orin, and I do, he wouldn't miss dinner for anything. Not sure about Sheila."

Turned out Sheila didn't want to miss dinner, either. She and Orin emerged from their room a couple of minutes after we knocked. I could tell the woman was braless but didn't mention it.

"I just couldn't, Annie," she whispered. "You know what I mean. I could barely get this blouse on and it's loose."

"I hear ya."

We followed behind our husbands down the narrow corridor. They seemed to forget that Sheila and I were handicapped by our burnt skin. Before long they were a couple hundred feet ahead of us. Oh well. We'd eventually catch up.

They did hold our spot at the elevator, thank goodness, and we climbed aboard. With so many people pressed in around me, touching my burnt arms, I couldn't help but cry out. This cleared a path in a hurry.

We entered the dining hall at exactly five-thirty and made our way to our table. Weirdly, no one from the wedding party showed up. Finally, at six-fifteen, Jake arrived, a panicked look on his face.

"Jake?" Warren stood to greet him. "Where is everyone?"

"They're still looking for Meredith. We were hoping she'd come here to dinner." He shook his head. "I. . .I. . ." He dropped down in a chair and the waiter filled his water glass. "I don't know what to think."

"Jake, there's got to be some mistake," Orin said. "Surely you don't think she's. . ."

"Gone?" Jake shook his head. "I can't come to any other conclusion."

"Did she give any indicators that she didn't want to get married?" I hated to ask the question, but the super-sleuth in me needed to get right to the point.

"No, she was so excited. You saw it for yourself. Everyone was." He paused and I could read the concern in his eyes. "Well, most everyone."

"Who? Who wasn't?" I asked.

"I, well. . .I don't think her mom was ready for Meredith to be away from home. They're in kind of a co-dependent relationship."

At this moment Kevin arrived, breathless. "She's not here?"

Jake shook his head. "No."

Kevin sat down and took a swig from Jake's water glass. "I've been everywhere, from the top deck to the bottom."

"Me too," Jake said. "Even went to the ship's security officer. He confirmed that she boarded. Her Set Sail pass was used to board and the passport was a perfect match. So, she's got to be here somewhere."

"Hiding from me, apparently." Jake took another roll and shoved it in his mouth.

"Relax, my friend." Kevin gave him a sympathetic look. "You never know with women. Maybe she's just panicked or having second thoughts or something."

"Is that supposed to make me feel better?"

"Jake, at least you know she's on-board," Warren gave him a

fatherly look.

"Right." The groom-to-be's brows elevated. "Only, not in her room, and not with anyone from the wedding party."

"Was she alone when she boarded?" I reached for the breadbasket but my burnt arm didn't extend as usual. Warren handed it to me.

Jake nodded. "They photograph everyone coming aboard. From what they could tell there was another woman in the distance but maybe not with her? I'm not sure."

"Probably her mom, right?" Sheila suggested. "Or your mom?"

"I've talked to both of them," Jake said. "They haven't seen her."

"Well, maybe it was Natalie, then?" I tried.

"She's the maid of honor, right?" Orin reached for a roll. "I'm having trouble keeping up with the players."

"Yes, she's the maid of honor, Orin." Sheila gave him a "be quiet" look.

"Natalie was with Jake's parents." Kevin took another swig of water.

"Ah." I took a bite out of my roll, deep in thought.

"I just don't get it," Kevin said. "The whole thing makes no sense."

It made no sense to me, either. Why would a bride deliberately miss her own wedding? I'd talked to her just this morning and she looked elated. She certainly didn't look like the sort to run and hide on her big day, and definitely not in a foreign country. Not that I could think clearly with this sunburn plaguing me. Right now I just wanted to dive face-first into the swimming pool and put an end to my misery.

A few minutes later Natalie showed up with the bride's mother. "No word?" she said.

Jake shook his head.

Don't Rock the Boat

The bride's mother started weeping and before long the waiter was seating everyone at our table and filling water glasses.

"I can't eat anything," Meredith's mother kept right on standing. "I might never eat again. I don't know how any of you can sit here when my daughter is missing. We've. Got. To. Do. Something!" She gave Jake a disgusted look and then turned and walked away from the table, muttering all the way.

"She's right." Jake shook his head. "I don't know where else to look but we have to try."

"Talk to the captain," I said. "He can put out a call for her. I heard him call for someone just last night, so I know it's possible."

"Oh, that's right." Momentary relief flickered in Jake's eyes. "I'll go find him. He rose and gazed at us all so intently I could feel his pain. "I know you guys are all Christians. I've heard you talk about going to church. Would you please pray? I don't know if Meredith is deliberately staying away from me because she doesn't want to marry me, or if someone's done her some sort of harm, but I know that praying is the answer."

"Of course," we all responded in unison.

Jake took off toward the dining room door and Kevin rose. He looked our way and sighed. "Thanks, everyone. I'd better stick with him. That's what the best man does. "

"Yes, and you're a great best man." I squirmed in my seat, the pain from my sunburn gripping me once again.

He took off and we sat quietly for a few minutes. The waiter finally broke the silence when he came to take our order. The next forty-five minutes were unbearable. I managed to swallow a few bites of food but couldn't stand the pain any longer. Sitting was miserable.

Turned out, standing was next-to-impossible. I figured that out when my husband and Orin rose to leave after dessert. My burnt thighs didn't want to cooperate. Looked like Sheila was having the same problem. She groaned and moaned as she attempted to get up from the chair. At that very moment, the whole ship started pitching back and forth, nearly causing us to tumble.

"Feels like we're setting off to sea again," Warren said. "Hope everyone's got their Dramamine."

I had some in the cabin, but right now I couldn't stand the idea of lying down in the bed, even as nauseous as I felt. I had to get in the water. Now.

"Sheila, come with me."

"Where are we going?"

"To the top deck. We're getting back in the pool."

"Right now?" Warren and Orin spoke in unison.

"Yep, right now."

"But I'm not in my bathing suit," Sheila argued. "And there's no way I could possibly get back into it, feeling like this."

"Exactly. Which is why we're going in in our clothes," I said.

"Is that even allowed?" Orin asked.

"I don't know and I don't care." And that was my final answer on the subject.

We got a few strange looks from people as we entered the pool in our sundresses but we ignored them and kept going. Our husbands settled into lounge chairs to watch the outdoor movie and I eased my way under the water, feeling the relief of the coolness against my skin.

"Do you think they'll let us sleep in here?" Sheila asked as she dipped her shoulders under.

"I don't know but that's the only thing that makes sense."

The ship jolted and the lights of the shore began to fade off in the distance. The events of the day all hit me at once, right about the time the nausea took hold. I did my best to hold my stomach contents in as I reflected on the day: the tour bus. The missing bride. The guy on the beach. Jake's frantic look. The maid of honor's strange countenance. The mother of the bride's anxieties. The best man's kindness. All of it sort of rolled together.

Or maybe it wasn't my thoughts rolling; maybe it was the ship. Yes, I could see people staggering about on the deck, a couple grabbing onto poles to keep from falling over.

"Annie, we've got to get back to the room." Warren's voice rang out. "It's starting to rain."

"It. . .it is?"

"And the wind is picking up," he added. "Do you need help out of the pool?"

Ugh. I did need help out. And I needed help getting back to the room. And help getting out of my wet dress. And help slathering on more Aloe Vera. And help getting into the loosest, most comfortable nightgown I owned. And help getting the covers down on the bed. And help easing myself into said bed. All of this, with the ship tipping this way and that.

Once in bed, I tried to get comfortable, but it was impossible. I must've moaned and groaned aloud because Warren sat next to me and gave me a sympathetic look. "Do you need something for pain?" he asked.

"If I took anything, it would come right back up."

"I can't believe I'm not feeling sick, with the boat rocking and rolling like this."

"Me either. I guess I'm the one with seasickness, not you."

An hour later I was still wide awake. Outside of our sliding glass door I could hear the wind howling. We might be on one of the largest ships in the Western Caribbean, but that didn't stop the winds from knocking us around like a toy ship in a bathtub. The ship bobbed this way and that, and the winds whistled an eerie tune that made my nausea more extreme.

"Why?" I cried out into the darkness. "Why didn't we get an interior room? At least the wind wouldn't keep us awake."

"I think the interior rooms might feel like the belly of a

whale," Warren answered. "Maybe it's better that we can see outside."

The piercing whistle of the wind nearly drowned out his words and the ship dipped to the right and then the left, a victim of the rocky seas.

"We. Are. Never. Doing. This. Again." I felt a lone tear roll down my cheek. It burned, causing even more pain. "Never. Ever. Ever."

In that moment, I thought about the missing bride. On a night like this, with the fierce winds blowing, I could picture someone losing their balance, tumbling off the side of the ship. I pinched my eyes shut and willed that thought away. Hopefully I would feel better by morning and could help Jake and the others figure this out. Right now. . .well, right now I just had to pray that sleep—merciful sleep—would come.

Chapter Seven

GIRL IN THE SEA

No vacation goes unpunished.
—Karl Hakkarainen

On Wednesday morning I awoke to find that my eyes wouldn't open. The swelling from the sunburn had sealed them shut. It took some doing on Warren's part, but after bringing me several wet compresses I was able to open them to tiny slits. I could see just enough outside our window to discover we'd docked in Grand Cayman. As if I could possibly get off the ship in this condition.

Warren insisted I see the ship's doctor. After consulting with Orin, it was decided Sheila should join me. So, off to the first deck we all went, two lobsters and their white-skinned mates. As we rounded the turn near the doctor's office, we ran into Kenzie once again. This time she was dressed in rehearsal clothes.

"Well, fancy meeting you here." She looked back and forth between Sheila and me. "Are you gals okay?"

"No," we both said in unison.

"Burnt to a crisp," I explained.

"I see that," she replied.

"And the motion of the ocean kept me up all night," Sheila added. "I was sick as a dog."

"If you think it's bad up on the passenger decks, you should try sleeping down here on the bottom. It's crazy." She wished us well and took off, but the strangest thought hit me. If Kenzie's room was down here in the bottom deck, why had we seen her getting off the elevator on the 10th deck yesterday afternoon?

Just as quickly I chastened myself. Probably searching for Meredith. Of course.

Then again, if she was so worried about Meredith, why didn't she mention her just now?

"A penny for your thoughts, Annie."

"Hmm?" I glanced over at Warren. Well, what I could see of Warren through the slits between my puffy eyelids, anyway. "What?"

"I know you, Annie Peterson. You're not solving this one. Let it go."

"Aye aye, Cap'n." I tried to salute, but—for obvious reasons—couldn't. Instead, I followed Warren into the sick bay where we waited to be seen.

The doctor, God bless him, couldn't do much except diagnose us with sunstroke and instruct us to stay lathered up with Aloe Vera and stay out of the sun. When we told him about our experience in the pool the night before, he laughed. "You're not the first and you won't be the last," he said. "But do yourselves a favor and skip whatever excursions you might've planned in Grand Cayman."

I hated to hear that news. We'd planned to do the pirate ship adventure.

After we left the sick bay, Sheila and I insisted the guys go on without us.

"No way am I leaving you in this condition, Annie," Warren said.

"But this is the excursion you were most excited about." I sighed. "Remember? You were dying to go on that pirate ship."

"Yeah, but it's not worth the risk of you staying alone."

"I won't be alone," I argued. "I've got Sheila."

"Yeah, she's got me," my lobster-esque best friend added. "And what kind of trouble would we get into, anyway? Neither of us can move."

"True." Warren looked Orin's way. "What do you think?"

"I think I'd like to get off this contraption and put my feet on dry land."

"So, go." Sheila gave him a "get out of here" look. "We'll be fine."

"Are you sure?" Warren looked my way.

"I'm sure. All I want to do is get back in the pool, anyway. If you guys come back and find us looking like prunes, you'll know why."

"Okay, okay."

And so it was agreed. We headed to the Windjammer for some breakfast then back to the cabin where the guys got their passports and headed out. After giving us another warning about taking it easy.

"I don't want to come back and find out you were solving any crimes, Annie." Warren gave me a "don't you dare" look and I shrugged. Well, I tried to shrug.

"Go on, Warren. And relax. Have a good time. . .for both of us."

"Okay, okay."

After he left, I joined Sheila in her room for a few minutes and then we both decided we'd be better off in the water. It took an act of Congress for both of us to get into our swimsuits, but we finally managed and then headed up to the top deck. Once there, I noticed the groom-to-be and the maid of honor seated next to each other on lounge chairs.

"Does that seem odd to you?" Sheila whispered.

"Maybe they're just comforting each other?" I had my doubts, though. "You can get in the water if you want. I think I'll ask about Meredith."

"Okay. Let me know."

Just as I walked toward Jake and Natalie, the band struck up a reggae number, which made it hard to talk. And hear.

"Any word?" I called out.

Jake shook his head. "No one has seen her. I talked to the Captain last night. They've been searching the ship all night. Did you hear him put out a call on the loudspeaker after dinner last night?"

"No. All I heard was the wind. I was kind of, well, sick."

"I see that." Natalie stared at me. "That's got to hurt."

"Yeah. I'm getting in the water. Want to join us?"

She shrugged. "Maybe in awhile. I'm pretty overwhelmed right now. Talking to Jake is helping."

She looked overwhelmed. Or distressed. I couldn't help but notice the red-rimmed eyes. Maybe she wasn't feeling well. I nodded and then wished them a good day as I headed off to join Sheila in the pool.

It felt fabulous. Absolutely, totally 'I-could-live-here-forever' fabulous.

We stayed in the pool for what felt like hours. Just as predicted, I felt my skin pruning. Still, I hated to get out. Besides, a super-sleuth could learn a lot from the pool area. Like, watching the maid of honor as she cozied up to the groom. Watching the mother of the bride as she passed by and observed the two of them together.

"Sheila," I whispered. "Look who's headed our way."

"Betsy." She spoke the woman's name aloud. "Yoo-hoo. Betsy. Mrs. Williams! Over here." She waved and the mother of the bride glanced our way. I could see the tension in her eyes as she saw us, but the woman still removed her cover-up, tossed it on a nearby lounge chair and then joined us in the pool.

Sheila, who never met a stranger, had no trouble engaging the woman in conversation. She started with the obvious. . .asking about Meredith. When Betsy shook her head in response, Sheila's eyes filled with tears, which seemed to endear her to the mother-of-the-bride-to-be, who started weeping.

I had the sense that Sheila would've wrapped her in a hug, had the situation been different. Instead, she lowered her voice, so the others in the pool wouldn't hear. "My heart is broken for you, Betsy," Sheila said. "Truly. And I want you to know that my husband and I have been praying for all of you from the very moment we heard the news. I won't stop, either. Not until she's standing in front of her groom in that beautiful chapel."

At once Betsy's tears dried up. Her expression shifted from sweetness to pain. The eerie silence on her end spoke volumes. She didn't want her daughter to marry Jake. That much was sure and certain.

After a couple moments of strained silence I cleared my throat. "Um, Betsy?"

"Yes?" She looked my way.

"I know we don't really know one another. Not really. So please forgive me if what I'm about to say is out of line."

Her brow wrinkled. "That might depend on what you're about to say."

"Right. Can I ask you a question?"

She shrugged. "Sure. I'm an open book."

I doubted that but didn't say so.

"Is Meredith your only daughter?"

It took a moment to nod and when she did her eyes filled with tears once more.

"And you're afraid of losing her?" I asked.

Betsy put her hands on the edge of the pool as if to steady

herself. "What does this have to do with anything? Of course I'm afraid of losing her, especially now that she's gone."

"I meant, are you afraid of losing her love, losing the relationship, once she and Jake get married."

Betsy clammed up. No response at all.

"I'm sorry," I managed after a moment's awkward pause. "I'm really not trying to get in your business." *Much.* "It's just that I've been a mother-of-the bride, too, and I know how depressing it can be, to think your daughter won't be your daughter in the same way after she's married. You know?" For whatever reason, I felt a catch in my throat as these words were spoken.

"I. Don't. Know." Betsy shook her head, tears now flowing. "She's my best friend. Always has been. She's my rock. And now she's. . .she's. . ."

"Starting a new life. And you're sad."

'Of course I'm sad, Betsy spouted. "It's only natural."

"Yes. Only natural."

Only, the look of anger that flashed in her eyes was anything but normal. Either this woman had serious issues with the groom-to-be or she simply didn't want to give up her daughter. Minutes later she excused herself and bounded from the pool. She grabbed her cover-up and took off at the speed of light. I turned back to Sheila, who seemed stumped by the woman's behavior.

"Was I out of line?" I asked. "I hope I didn't hurt her feelings."

"It was just a mother to mother talk, but I'm guessing she's overly sensitive right now." Sheila dunked her shoulders under the water again. "You know?"

"Right." A pause followed as I watched Betsy disappear through the glass doors toward the elevators. "But what if. . ." I released a slow breath as I tried to figure out how to finish my thought aloud.

"What if. . .what?" Sheila asked.

"What if she had something to do with her own daughter's disappearance?"

"Huh? What do you mean?"

"I mean, she's not happy about her daughter's marriage, so maybe she spirited her away to her own cabin yesterday. Maybe all of this 'Where is my daughter?' stuff is just an act. You know?"

"You're saying she might be holding her own daughter captive in her cabin?" Sheila pursed her lips. "Annie, that's crazy, even for you."

"Thanks a lot."

"Oh, c'mon. You know what I mean. Besides, how would she manage that?"

"She'd need help." I stopped to think about it. "Her husband is traveling with her but you hardly see them together. Maybe he's in the room with Meredith right now." I paused, deep in thought. "Does he look the sort to hold his daughter captive?"

"He looked perfectly normal," Sheila said.

"Those are the worst kinds," I was quick to add. "The perfectly normal looking ones, I mean."

"Annie, you've lost it."

Okay, I had to admit, that whole mother-of-the-bride-kidnaps-her-daughter-to-keep-her-from-getting-married bit was a bit of a stretch, but stranger things had happened.

"I'm more inclined to think the maid of honor is no true friend." Sheila's eyes narrowed to slits as she looked at Natalie. Okay, they were already narrowed to slits from the swelling but she did seem more concerned than usual as she glanced the maid of honor's way. "Do you see how close she's sitting to Jake? Seems. . .weird."

"Well, since you brought that up, I need to tell you something," I said.

"Oh?"

"Remember that first night, when we walked the deck after dinner?"

"The night that Warren and Orin declared their undying love to one another?" she giggled.

"Yes. That night." I paused and gave Natalie and Jake another look. "I didn't want to say anything at the time but. . ." I lowered my voice and leaned her way. "I saw Jake and Natalie together."

"*Together* together?"

"Well, not kissing or anything. But they were close. In the moonlight. Whispering. You know? It struck me as odd."

"That *is* very odd." She gave them another look. "But maybe they were cooking up some sort of surprise for Meredith."

"Some sort of kidnapping, you mean?"

Sheila shook her head. "Annie, are you saying you think Jake is in on this now?"

"I don't know what I'm saying. I think I'm delirious." I certainly felt that way. My head was pounding.

"Too much chlorine. We need to get out of here and find some lunch."

We somehow hobbled out of the pool just as Natalie and Jake took off toward the Windjammer. I couldn't manage the whole drying off with a towel thing, so I just slipped on my cover-up and Sheila and I headed over to the snack bar to get a burger. We settled in at a nearby table and ate burgers and fries. After a while I almost forgot about my sunburn. Almost.

I happened to glance up at the television screen overhead just as we finished eating and noticed a promo for the spa. Man, didn't that look awesome. A day at the spa? Sounded terrific. Well, not terrific right now, with a sunburn, of course.

Just then I caught a glimpse of something—er, someone—familiar on the screen. I gasped aloud and Sheila looked my way.

"Sheila, look." I pointed at the screen. They're doing an advertisement for the spa. But look. That woman in the chair... the one getting the facial. Isn't that Meredith?"

Sheila squinted at the screen. "I think so. I can't make out her face but I'd recognize those earrings anywhere. She was wearing them that first night at dinner." This led to a lengthy conversation from Sheila about how she never forgot a great pair of earrings.

"If that's really Meredith in the spa, then our question is answered once and for all," I said. "She's on the ship and she's fine."

"But why would she go to the spa, right there in broad daylight, if she's hiding from people?"

"I don't know, Sheila. But we've got to get down there and ask them. Maybe she's there now. Maybe that was live footage."

"Well, what are we waiting for? Let's hit the road." Sheila looped her arm through mine, as if to hurry me along. Instead, she let out a yelp as her burnt skin touched mine. I hollered out in pain at the very same time. Unfortunately, everyone within a dozen feet turned and looked at us. I doubled over in pain.

A young man approached with a worried expression. "Everything okay over here?"

"I. . .I. . ." I couldn't quite answer. Not yet.

"Did she hit you, Ma'am?" The fellow glared at Sheila.

I managed to stand aright and shook my head. "No. Nothing like that. She just. . .touched me."

"Touched you?" His gaze narrowed.

"Great, Annie. Get me arrested on battery charges." Sheila groaned. "That's all I need. Throw my tail in the pokey when I'm burnt to a crisp. Wouldn't that be fun?"

Didn't sound like fun to me. The only thing that sounded any good at all was getting back into the pool, but we didn't have time for that right now.

The young man kept staring at me, as if waiting for an

explanation.

"My sunburn," I explained. "She touched my sunburn. She was trying to help, not hurt."

"If you're sure." He looked at Sheila as if he didn't quite believe my story.

"I'm clean, officer." Sheila put her hands up in the air. "You can search me, but the only thing you'll find is a bunch of wrinkles tightly squished down by a Lycra bathing suit that's two sizes too small."

I actually laughed out loud at that. The young man didn't find it quite as entertaining. He shook his head, then turned and walked away, muttering something about old women.

"Really?" Sheila put her arms down. "Did he really just call us old?"

"He did, Sheila." I sighed. "But don't get too worked up about it. To someone that age we probably do seem old."

"Speak for yourself, Annie Peterson. We're as young as we feel." The stubbornness on her face convinced me she felt young. Me? Not so much.

"Right now, with this sunburn, I feel like an arthritic old woman who can barely move," I said. "Now, let's get out of here before I drag you back into the pool. I want to make it to the spa before the sun goes down."

She paused and gave me a curious look. "It's only two-thirty."

"Exactly. Better get going."

Thank goodness we didn't have far to go. It turned out the spa was on the same floor, just inside the glass doors by the elevator on the aft end. When we got to the front and asked about Meredith, the receptionist—a woman with a strong Russian accent—refused to give us any information.

"I can't give *zee* customer's infor-*may*-see-on."

"But this is a special situation," I explained. "This is a woman who's missing."

The receptionist narrowed her gaze and stared at me as if she thought I was dense. "*Zat* makes no sense at all. *Eef* she *eez* mesing, *az* you say, *how* can she be in *zee* salon? She put her hands on her hips, as if in a showdown of wills.

"Right, right. I see your dilemma." I looked at Sheila, hoping she could help.

My friend leaned forward and put her palms on the reception desk. "Look, sister. We know you're not supposed to give private information, but this is a woman whose life could be in danger."

"*Vee* place no one's life in danger in *zee* salon, I can assure you of *zat*."

"Got it." Sheila rolled her eyes. "I'm not accusing you. I'm telling you that this is a woman who is in danger. Elsewhere. So if she's here we really need to know."

"I cannot give out any personal in-for-*may*-see-on."

"Mm-hmm." Sheila leaned forward and whispered. "What's it gonna take, sister? How much money are we talking to get this dam to break?"

"Sheila!" I gasped aloud. Surely she wasn't bribing the woman, right?"

"*Vhat*?" The receptionist looked stunned.

"I'm sorry, Ma'am. Please excuse my friend. She has a case of sunstroke. The doctor confirmed it this morning. I think it's messed with her head." I glared at Sheila.

"There's nothing wrong with my head," Sheila said. "And my offer still stands."

"Ugh. Sheila!"

Just when I started to turn around the receptionist cleared her throat. "Perhaps I *might* know this woman of which you speak."

"Ah ha. I thought so." Sheila gave her a pensive look. "Spill the beans, if you please. We don't have all day."

"And *vhat* do I get in return?"

Sheila paused and I could practically hear the wheels clacking in her head. "You get me, not telling your boss that you almost accepted a bribe."

"Sheila!" I glared at her once again.

"I *vill* call my manager at once." The woman's gaze narrowed. "Perhaps she will help you."

Turned out the manager, a large Swedish woman, was more open to conversation once she heard ship security was involved. She flipped through the schedule and then shook her head. "I don't see anyone named Meredith on today's schedule."

"What about yesterday?" Sheila asked.

"She was with us at the beach yesterday, Sheila," I said. "Not here."

"I don't see her on yesterday's schedule, anyway," the manager said. "Let me check Monday." A couple of minutes later we had our answer. "Yes, here she is. We saw her at one o'clock on Monday afternoon. I remember her now. She's the one who was getting married the following night in the chapel."

"Only, she didn't," I said. "She hasn't been seen since Tuesday afternoon in Cozumel."

The receptionist clucked her tongue. "Mexico *eez* dangerous."

"Actually, there's a record of her coming back on-board the ship," Sheila explained. So maybe *zee* ship *eez* dangerous."

I would've jabbed my friend in the ribs as a punishment for her rudeness but the pain to my burnt elbow wouldn't have been too much to handle.

The manager gave Sheila a confused look. "I do remember now. The camera crew stopped by on Monday to film their advertisement for the spa. They must've come while Meredith was here."

"I guess that makes sense." It disappointed me, of course, but answered the "When did she go to the spa?" question.

I thanked the manager for her time and she disappeared down the hallway.

Sheila turned back toward the elevator. "Let's get out of here, Annie. I'm in a lot of pain."

"*Vee* have a mud bath to help *zee* sunburn," the receptionist said. "Half price for senior citizens."

Sheila grunted and took off for the elevators. I turned back and shrugged. "Not today, thanks."

The woman mumbled something under her breath. Still, what was up with the senior citizens comment? Did everyone on-board *Navigator of the Seas* think we were elderly?

I caught a glimpse of my reflection in the mirrored doors at the elevator. With the sunburn, every wrinkle in my elderly face seemed exaggerated. No wonder.

Well, I'd prove them wrong. I'd prove them all wrong. This old lady would be back up and running in no time. And I'd find that bride, too, if it was the last thing I did.

Chapter Eight

MOONLIGHT ON WATER

At sea, I learned how little a person needs, not how much.
—Robin Lee Graham

When our guys returned from the pirate ship adventure we dressed for dinner and headed down to the dining room. No one in the bridal party showed up, which threw me a little. Maybe they had decided to take all of their meals in the Windjammer. Maybe—just maybe—one or more of them was deliberately avoiding us.

"Annie, are you with us?" Warren spoke above the noise in the dining room.

"Hmm? What?"

"I was telling you about the pirate ship excursion. You would've loved it, Annie. Right up your alley."

"Yeah, they made some of the people walk the plank and everything." Orin laughed. "And they even tied this one guy up to the mast pole and poured a bucket of ice on him."

"Then they made the kids swab the decks." Warren couldn't stop laughing. "Tell her about that one kid, Orin."

"The one with the attitude?" Orin chuckled. "They ended up

dressing him in a pirate costume and commissioning him to work on-board the *Esmeralda*. That's the name of the pirate ship, by the way."

"So, they didn't deputize either of you?" Sheila asked. "Cause if either one of you have converted to the pirate's way of life, you'd better let us know."

"Nah. My stomach couldn't take life on the sea." Warren reached for the bread basket and a pat of butter. "The *Esmeralda* was rockier than the *Navigator*, even at its worst. And that's saying a lot."

"That is saying a lot," I agreed. "Last night was awful."

"Well, I'm glad you made it home safely." Sheila took a sip of her tea. "We had a few adventures today, too, but nothing like that."

Warren looked my way and I just shrugged. "Sheila bribed a woman in the spa."

"You did?" Orin gave her an admiring look. "That's my girl. Did you get a free massage out of the deal?"

"Nah. I'm too burnt for a massage." She set her tea glass down. "Maybe when I'm feeling better."

"Well, speaking of feeling better. . ." My husband gave me a compassionate look. "If you still aren't feeling well tomorrow, we can just skip the excursion in Jamaica."

"No!" Sheila and I spoke the word simultaneously.

"I've been dying to go to Dunn's River Falls," I said. "Ever since I looked it up online. It's beautiful. Absolutely beautiful. And I want to see it in person. This might be the only time in my life I get to do so, you know?"

"Okay, if you're sure. But I'm going to put my foot down about you climbing the falls. You're in no shape to do that."

"Thanks a lot."

"You know what I mean, Annie."

"Okay, okay. No climbing for me. I'll just look as others

climb."

"Me too," Sheila chimed in.

"Me too," Orin added. "Don't think I'm up for it."

No doubt. The poor guy was barely past his chemo, after all. He'd done well to do the pirate ship excursion today.

"What about you, Warren?" I asked. "Are you wanting to climb the falls or just go as a sightseer?"

He shrugged. "I guess I'll make up my mind tomorrow."

We spent the rest of the dinner hour engaged in conversation about our day. Warren didn't seem terribly pleased that I'd gotten involved in the missing bride story, but didn't say anything to put a stop to my ponderings. He knew me well, that Warren.

"Annie, I know your heart," he said as we wrapped up our dessert. "You want the best for everyone. God put that inside of you, so who am I to argue with it?"

"I just want to see her returned. . .and happy." A shrug followed as I thought about the blissful look on Meredith's face just a few days ago. "I'd want that for my own girls. You know?"

"I know." He shrugged. "So, what's next?"

"I have to figure out if the mother of the bride might be up to tricks."

"Annie, that's just silly. A mother doesn't kidnap her own daughter."

"I wouldn't be so sure. Did you see that one Dateline episode? The one about the girl in Oregon? Her parents kept her locked up from the time she was a little girl."

"I saw that episode." Sheila took another nibble of her chocolate pie.

"They were psychopaths." Warren quirked a brow.

"Exactly! So, one never knows. Psychopaths could be walking among us."

I didn't realize the waiter was standing behind me until he cleared his throat. "I've been accused of many things in my life,

Don't Rock the Boat

but I've never been called a psychopath before."

I turned to face him and smiled. "Oh, you're no psychopath. You've been the best waiter ever. You're like one of the family now."

This led to a lengthy discussion about his family in Thailand.

After we finished eating, Sheila and I headed off to the ladies room to freshen up for the big show in the theater. I'd been waiting for the 50s show all week, so tonight would prove to be fun. I hoped. If I could stop thinking about the conversation I'd had with Mrs. Williams earlier today. And the tears coming from Natalie as she talked to Jake on the upper deck. Sheila and I stared at our burnt faces in the mirror for a couple of minutes, talked about how awful we looked, then, convinced there was nothing we could do about it, decided to touch up our lipstick. Afterwards we left the teensy-tiny bathroom to see if our husbands were ready for a walk down the Promenade deck.

We found them seated on a bench, looking pretty wiped out.

Sheila laughed when she saw them. "Too much food, fellas?"

Warren nodded, but I could see the concern in his eyes as he silently gestured to Orin, who didn't look well.

"Maybe we should skip the show?" Warren suggested. "It's been a long day."

"No way." Orin rose—slowly—and plastered on what looked to be a strained smile. "My girl's been looking forward to 50s night all week. So have I." He started to loop his arm through Sheila's, but then looked at her burnt skin. "Oops. Sorry."

We walked from one end of the Promenade deck to the other. When we reached the theater, we realized we were early. Really, really early. The show wasn't scheduled to start until eight o'clock. It was just now six forty-five.

"I say we walk off some of this food." Orin rubbed his belly. "I think I've gained ten pounds over the past three or four days."

"Are you sure you're up for a walk, Orin?" I could read the

concern in Sheila's eyes. "You don't want to sit in the café and have some decaf coffee or something?"

"I'm up for it. I've been wanting to see the library. And the chapel. We never made it up there, since the wedding was, well..."

"Right. Well, let's go for a walk, then." I took my husband's extended hand—grateful it didn't hurt—and we took off on an adventure around the ship. As always, Sheila got us turned around. Every time we came to a fork in the road, she advised us to go the wrong way.

"You've got your aft and your forward mixed up," Warren explained.

"Nothing new there." Sheila laughed.

Before long we found the library, filled with all sort of people playing cards and board games.

"Now there's a good idea." Sheila pointed at a wall filled with books and games. "On Friday and Saturday when we have nothing else to do, we can come up here and play games. Or cards."

Sounded like fun. Well, until I remembered what a serious game-player Orin was. He didn't like to lose. Hmm.

After visiting the library we finally located the skylight chapel—up, up, up above most everything else on the ship. The room was small, but pretty. I sat on one of the benches and Warren took a seat next to me. Orin plopped down on my husband's right, but Sheila—sweet Sheila—paced around and commented on everything—the stained glass, the various architectural features. Everything.

"I think this wood is fake." She pointed to an altar. "Kind of tacky, don't you think?"

So much for a peaceful, spiritual moment.

We were interrupted by something else, too. From a little side room just off the chapel—a prayer room of some sort—I heard someone weeping. The others heard it, too. I couldn't help myself. I had to see if that someone—whoever he or she was—needed our help. I rose and tiptoed to the entrance of the dark room and peeked inside.

I saw a woman—well, a woman's back, anyway. I couldn't really tell much about her, except that she appeared to be weeping. Her brown hair put me in mind of someone right away, but I wasn't sure who.

I took Sheila's hand and tugged her away from the entrance, then whispered, "Do you have your camera?"

"My camera? Sure." She reached into her tiny purse and came out with her smart phone. "Why?"

"You can zoom in, right?"

"Sure."

"Just act like you're taking pictures of the chapel, but zoom in on the woman to see if she's familiar."

"Take her picture?" Sheila's hoarse whisper was a bit too loud.

I shook my head. "No."

Our husbands took off for the outer hall. Cowards. Sheila and I made our way—on tiptoes—back to the prayer room entrance, where we heard the weeping continue.

Sheila zoomed in on the woman until we saw something startling.

The earrings.

The earrings.

I did my best not to gasp aloud. I grabbed Sheila's hand and pulled her out of the chapel into the hall with the guys.

"Was that who I think it was?" My best friend's eyes widened. "I'd recognize those earrings anywhere."

"Who?" Warren looked confused.

"What earrings?" Orin echoed.

The bride was wearing a certain pair of earrings that first

night at dinner. I remember commenting on them," Sheila whispered.

Warren's eyes widened. "What do we do now?"

"We, um. . ." I looked around and noticed the ladies room across from the chapel. "We wait in here until she comes out."

"All of us?" Orin looked terrified by this prospect.

"Sure. We're the only ones on this floor," Sheila said. "No one is going to see you."

Warren shook his head. "But. . ."

He didn't have time to finish. We heard the woman walking toward us and we flew into action. Warren opened the bathroom door and we all rushed inside. When we realized the woman was coming into the ladies room, Warren and Orin headed into one stall, and Sheila and I headed into another. That left only one empty stall.

We heard the click, click, click of the woman's heels as they made their way across the marble floor. She entered the empty stall, and the sound of her sniffles continued. After a moment she grew silent. I tried to figure out what to do, but couldn't think clearly. Then again, that might have something to do with the fact that Sheila had climbed up onto the toilet.

From the next stall the woman's voice sounded. "Do you... do you have any toilet paper over there, by any chance?"

I collected a wad of paper and shoved it under the partition that separated us.

"Thank you."

I strained to make out the voice. It didn't really sound like the bride. But. . .those earrings. Sheila swore they were the same.

At this point I decided to do the unthinkable. I had to exit my stall, as if nothing unusual was going on, walk to the sink and wash my hands. That was the only way I'd ever see this woman face to face. And I had to do all of this without Sheila being seen. Oh, and without the guys being discovered in the third stall.

I pulled open my door and stepped out just as I heard the flush coming from the woman's stall next to me. I closed the door behind me and prayed Sheila would stay put up on the toilet. When I reached the sink, I heard the woman's stall door open and I glanced into the mirror to catch a glimpse of the reflection.

"Mrs. Peterson?"

I turned to face Natalie. Not the bride-to-be. "Well, hello, honey. Fancy meeting you here."

"I was just. . ." She paused and tears welled in her eyes. "I was just in the chapel. I have so much on my mind. I just needed to be away from everyone."

"I understand, trust me." I understood part of it, anyway.

I turned my focus to the mirror once again and reached for my purse to pull out my lipstick tube. As Natalie washed her hands, I followed her reflection in the mirror. The swollen eyes. The tear-stained cheeks. This was a woman in distress. But I couldn't get past the sensation that she had more on her mind than just a missing friend.

As she reached for a paper towel, I garnered the courage to ask a question. "Beautiful earrings, Natalie. I love them."

"Thank you." She fingered them. "Meredith gave them to me. We have a matching set. We were supposed to wear them at the…" She began to cry in earnest now. "At. . .the. . .wedding." A sob followed. Then she finally caught her breath and added, "Which. Didn't. Happen!" More tears came on the tail end of this.

Hmm. Maybe I'd better lay my suspicions aside and just comfort this young woman.

"I have an idea, Natalie. It's just you and me here." Sort of. "Let's go back in the chapel for a minute and pray for Meredith… together. The Bible says there's power when people pray together. What do you think?"

She nodded and, for the first time, offered a faint smile. "I have so much to pray about Mrs. Peterson. You have no idea."

"Well, we'll start with Meredith and go from there, okay?"

She nodded and then walked toward the door. As we stepped out into the hall I prayed Sheila and the guys would take the hint and scurry on down the hallway to the stairs to wait on me. I went into the chapel to discover a very large, loud family had entered to take pictures. Natalie and I did our best to pray together, but the noise made it difficult, so we barely got a few words out about Meredith before an elderly woman asked us to snap some photos. I did so, and then left Natalie alone in the room, at her request. I guess she needed more time.

I tore down the hallway and found my husband and friends in the stairwell.

"It was Natalie," I said.

"Figured that out for myself, Annie." Sheila rolled her eyes. "You don't have to be a super-sleuth to stand on a toilet and listen to a conversation."

"I learned a lot, myself." Orin's eyes widened. "I learned that the ladies rooms are a lot nicer than the men's rooms."

The chuckle that followed eased the tension. We headed to the elevators and went down to the Promenade deck, then made our way to the theater. Unfortunately, so much time had passed we couldn't find good seats. We had to watch the 50s review from the far left side. Still, I was close enough to see Kenzie dressed in her poodle skirt. And when she sang *"A Whole Lotta Shakin' Goin' On"* we didn't even have to use our imaginations. The ship was, once again, rocking and rolling as we pulled away from the Bahamas and out to sea.

Hopefully more clues would come tomorrow in Jamaica. For now, I settled back against my seat and hummed along, my toes tapping all the while.

Chapter Nine

DON'T FIGHT THE SEA

There is nothing more enticing, disenchanting, and enslaving than the life at sea.
—Joseph Conrad

On Thursday we got off the ship in Jamaica. Sheila and I faced a huge dilemma: sunblock caused a burning sensation on our already burnt skin. In the end, we both coated ourselves in Aloe Vera and put on long-sleeve shirts and pants. We also wore huge straw hats so that our faces stood no chance of seeing any sunlight first-hand.

"You look like a tourist," Warren said as we boarded the bus in to go to Dunn's River Falls.

"Oh well. I am a tourist. I might as well look the part."

Just before the bus took off, someone familiar climbed aboard. I smiled when I saw the best man.

"Well, hello." He stopped by our row to offer a smile. "Looks like I'll have friends nearby."

"Definitely." I nodded. "You going to climb the falls?"

"Yep. Tried to talk Kenzie into going but she's so busy with rehearsals and all."

"How are things, well, how are things going?" Warren asked.

Kevin shrugged. "I don't know. For some reason Jake isn't speaking to me today. He's acting so odd." Kevin leaned down to whisper, "Does anyone else but me wonder if he's up to something? I mean, he's my best friend, but the way he's acting this week has me so confused. I know he's hurting but I just wonder. . ." Kevin's words drifted off.

Before I could say, "I've been wondering the very same thing," the tour guide's voice came over the loudspeaker, asking all passengers to take their seats. Kevin shrugged and trucked to the back of the bus where he sat next to an elderly man, who'd fallen asleep in his seat.

At this point, a female tour guide boarded the bus. She put us through several rounds of "Don't worry, be happy!" and then we were on our way.

Well, on our way until we got about halfway there. Then I heard a popping sound and the bus began to hobble along. The driver pulled over and the tour guide went up to ask him what had happened. She reappeared with a rousing, "Don't worry! Be happy!" and then proceeded to tell us we'd had a blowout. Another bus was on the way.

Only, the other bus didn't come. Not for a while, anyway. The tour guide's over-the-top smile and bright personality faded more with each passing minute and her true personality came out when people asked to get off the bus to wait in a nearby parking lot.

"Tragedy brings out the worst in some people, I guess," Sheila muttered from the seat behind us. "Folks aren't always what they pretend to be."

"No, indeed. And I had to wonder, based on what Kevin had just told me, if the groom-to-be was who he pretended to be. Had he been stringing Meredith along for some reason? Why pretend to want to marry her, and then get rid of her just before the wedding? It made no sense."

Then again, none of this made sense. And things got even more nonsensical as the clocked ticked away the minutes and we sat on the hot bus.

Miss Don't-Worry-Be-Happy finally agreed that we could get off and stand in the parking lot when one of the older ladies complained the heat was making her nauseous. Minutes later we exited the bus and ended up in a parking lot. I could hear the tour guide on the phone, yelling at someone on the other end. Yep. The happy-go-lucky persona was just that—a persona. Not the real deal.

Only, I'd fallen for it, hadn't I? Those happy-go-lucky types were often up to something.

Hmm. Kevin was a happy-go-lucky type, wasn't he? Maybe he had something to do with this. Maybe he made up that story about the groom just to divert us. Maybe—

"Annie?" Warren gave me a strange look.

"What?"

"You're not with us, are you?"

"Of course I'm with you. I'm standing in a stinky parking lot in front of a broken-down bus in beautiful Jamaica, wondering how long it's going to take before we're rescued." *And wondering how long it's going to take before a certain bride-to-be is rescued. Or if she will ever be rescued.*

"I know you, Annie. You're here in body, but not in spirit." He gave me a knowing look.

"I'm just thinking, Warren. Nothing wrong with that."

"Unless it lands you in trouble. So, stop thinking, Annie. Just relax and enjoy yourself. We're in Jamaica."

"Right." I looked around the icky parking lot, beyond the stack of old tires, past the broken-down sign in front of a nearby store and happened to notice Kevin, talking on his cell phone.

"Ooo, they have cell service?" I reached for my beach bag

and pulled out my phone. I'm going to call Candy."

"It'll cost a fortune from here, Annie," Sheila said.

"I don't care. I want to make sure she's okay. Make sure she hasn't had the baby yet."

The minute I turned on my phone, three text messages came through from Candy. They'd obviously been sent on Sunday, looking at the date on them. The first was a picture of Sasha. The second, a picture of Copper. The third, a very pregnant Candy, holding one dog in each arm.

"Well, I don't think it's very wise for her to be lifting those heavy dogs while she's pregnant," I said. "I need to tell her to take it easy."

Warren rolled his eyes. "Annie, she's a big girl."

"Yes." I looked at her blossoming belly. "She is, at that."

I placed the call and spent a few minutes laughing and talking with Candy, who definitely had not had the baby yet. She even put the phone on speaker so Sasha and Copper could hear my voice. They responded with yipping and yapping, clearly excited.

When I ended the call I had tears in my eyes and a lump in my throat.

"Is something wrong, Annie?" Sheila asked.

"No." I shoved my phone back in my bag. "I just miss them, is all."

"You were dying to go on this cruise, remember?" Warren crossed his arms at his chest. "You said it was going to be the experience of a lifetime."

"Well, it's definitely that." I looked out toward the road just as another bus pulled up. Kevin didn't seem to notice, so I walked his way to let him know. When I got close he quickly ended his call, pressed his phone into his back pocket and followed me onto the new bus. Well, new to us. Turned out it was a pretty old, run-down bus. And our lovely tour guide grew more sour by the moment.

Don't Rock the Boat

As we drove toward Dunn's River Falls, I couldn't control my wandering thoughts. The missing bride. The groom and maid of honor. The emotional mother-of-the-bride. The best man with the pink sparkly cell phone.

Pink. Sparkly. Cell phone.

Weird. But there it was, a flash of reality. He'd pressed a pink, sparkly cell phone into his back pocket. Very, very odd.

Or not. Maybe he'd borrowed Kenzie's cell phone to use in Jamaica. Yes, surely that was it. The girl had a lavish tattoo, after all, Maybe she liked over-the-top things like pink sparkly phone cases.

I put all thoughts of the MIA bride out of my mind when we got to Dunn's River Falls. We walked the path along the falls, watching as dozens—no, hundreds—of people climbed up, up, up. Any other time I might've joined them, but not this time. Not with this sunburn.

"Wishing you could do that?" Sheila asked.

I gazed into her burnt face and smiled. "Well, I suppose. Or maybe I'm happy for the excuse not to have to. Looks slippery. And dangerous."

"A little danger is good for the soul." She grinned. "If I didn't have this sunburn, I'd be first in line to sign up for this. Life is short. There are only so many adventures, and I want to be front and center for all of them."

Indeed, she did.

We lingered at the edge of the falls, watching people climb, climb, climb. We didn't know any of them, of course. Until Sheila happened to see our friend, Kevin.

"Yoo-hoo! Kevin!" She called out his name and he glanced our way, then smiled and gave us a wave. Sheila snapped a photo of him. She happened to catch a shot of him slipping and nearly falling.

"Don't distract him, Sheila," Orin said. "Don't want the poor fella to break his neck so you can get a great shot."

"True, true." She showed up the photo. "But I did get a good one, didn't I? Do you think he'll mind if I post this to Facebook?"

"Not from here, please," Orin said. "It'll cost you a fortune for Wi-Fi."

"Okay, okay. I'll post it when we get back home," Sheila said. "I can't wait to show everyone what a great time we've had."

"Great time?" Warren laughed. "Which part? The sunburn? The missing bride? The broken-down-bus?"

"All of it." My best friend's eyes filled with tears as she shoved her phone back into her bag. "Several months ago, when Orin was going through chemo, I didn't know if we'd ever get to take a trip like this. So, this one will be a memory-maker. Who knows if we'll ever pass this way again."

Oooh, I wanted to give her a hug, right then and there. Stupid sunburn! Instead, I gave her a broad smile and stared into her tear-filled eyes. Who, indeed, knew if we'd ever pass this way again? Some journeys in life were meant to be taken only once, after all. I would do my best to lay down my anxieties about the missing bride and focus on what was right in front of me—my husband and my friends.

Chapter Ten

THIS OCEAN

"Eat well, travel often."

After re-boarding the ship in Jamaica we said our goodbyes to excursions and settled in for the long trip back to Galveston. We had two more days at sea ahead of us and I didn't want to miss a minute with Warren, Sheila and Orin. Following a hunch—if one could call it that—I used our onboard credit for Internet access. I needed to do a bit of super-sleuthing. After fifteen minutes I gave up, more confused than ever.

Warren and I played cards with Sheila and Orin on Friday morning in the library and then ate lunch at the Windjammer. Out of the corner of my eye I noticed Natalie, Jake and the whole wedding party.

Well, most of the wedding party. Kevin was still missing from the group. Why had Jake turned him away? I made up my mind to stop thinking about it, if I could.

So, I tried.

I tried as we played miniature golf at 2:30.

I tried when Sheila and I ate an ice cream cone around four

o'clock while our husbands snoozed in the cabins below.

I tried extra hard when I passed Kevin and Kenzie in the hall on my way back to the cabin before dinner.

I tried as we ate dinner at our table with Jake and Natalie joining us. Alone.

I tried and tried all night long as I tossed and turned in the bed, the waves knocking the *Navigator of the Seas* around like a bar of soap in a bathtub.

But, try as I may, I couldn't stop thinking about Meredith. When I awoke Saturday morning it was all I could do not to say something to Warren. He must've picked up on my anxieties some time after breakfast. We'd just returned to our cabin when he gave me that 'I-know-you're-up-to-something' look.

"What is it, Annie?"

"Nothing."

"Mm-hmm. You've got something on your mind."

I shrugged.

"Well, you need a distraction. Want to go to the library to read a book?"

"Are you kidding me?" I asked. "Remember how loud it was in the library yesterday? There were at least thirty people playing some sort of dice game. I couldn't hear myself think, let alone read."

"Ah. Well, what about the café down on five? We could read there. Or just drink another cup of coffee."

"Loud music. The rhythm bothers me."

"Okay then, how about up on eleven? By the pool?"

"The glare is a problem with my e-reader. Can't read a word in the sunlight."

"There's that Solarium area," he suggested. "It's covered. They have those nice lounge chairs."

"And it's impossible to get one of them. Have you been up there? Every single chair is taken. If you're not there by seven-thirty in the morning, you don't get one."

"So, what are you saying?"

"Warren, I hope you'll forgive me in advance, but I have something else altogether that I want to do today and I'm hoping—no, I'm praying—you'll go along with it."

"Annie? What are you up to?"

"Warren, I want you to come with me to the ship's security office."

"Security office?"

"Well, I don't really know if that's what it's called but wherever we go to ask about a missing bride."

"Annie, they've already searched the ship. They've even called in the Coast Guard, remember? There's no sign of her."

"I know, Warren." I sat on the edge of the bed and sighed. "But something is nagging at me and I can't let it go. Remember they said she was photographed coming aboard that day in Cozumel?"

"Right."

"I want to see that photo."

"Why?" His brow wrinkled.

"I don't know. I'm just playing a hunch. But I have to see that photo."

"All right, Agatha Annie." He extended his hand. "Do you want your side-kick to come with us?"

"Mm-hmm."

"Well, c'mon then. Time's a wastin'."

I threw my arms around his neck, realizing that my sunburn barely hurt anymore. "Thank you, thank you. Let's get this show on the road."

Minutes later we stood in Sheila and Orin's room, explaining my prompting to talk to the people in security. My BFF said, "I thought you'd never ask," then reached for her phone. "In case you need my photographic skills," she said. "This phone has an excellent camera, remember?"

It took a bit of doing to figure out where to go, but the folks at the front desk referred us to the security department. The officer needed a bit of persuasion but finally agreed to let us look at the photo of Meredith once we explained we were friends of the family.

As soon as I saw the picture of Meredith, my heart lurched. I hadn't prepared myself for the frightened look on her face. This wasn't our smiling, happy bride-to-be. This was a woman terrified by her situation. But, why?

I squinted, trying to get a better look at the screen. "She is alone, right?"

"Looks like it." The officer zoomed in on a passenger behind her. "This is one of our crew members. I can tell from the uniform."

"Uniform?"

"Right. Many of our regular crew members work with the photographers in port. They all wear a certain uniform for when it's their turn to do that."

"I see." So, Meredith had come back through alone, with only a crewmember behind her. No one in the bridal party. Very strange, indeed.

"Did you get your questions answered, Annie?" Sheila asked.

I sighed and shook my head. "No. And I feel like a fool for getting everyone's hopes up. I was sure I'd see something that would trigger a thought, a memory, an idea."

"It's okay, honey." Warren gave me a compassionate look. "Can we just agree to put all of this behind us and let the proper authorities take it from here?"

I wanted to agree, but couldn't manage anything more than a grunt.

We left the office and headed up to the café for a cup of coffee. It had to be more than a coincidence that we landed at a

Don't Rock the Boat

table next to Natalie and Jake, who appeared to be in a quiet conversation. A little too quiet. A little too close, too.

Apparently we weren't the only ones who thought so. A couple of minutes later the bride's parents approached. They took one look at Jake and turned on their heels, as if to leave. I called out to them and they stopped.

"Please join us," I said. "We'd love to have you."

Sheila and Orin moved their chairs over to make room and, with a sigh, Betsy and her husband joined us. I could tell they were uncomfortable around Jake and Natalie, though.

"We'd hate to interrupt anything personal." Betsy's words were directed at me, but her gaze was on Jake and Natalie.

"I promise, this is not what you think." Jake pinched his eyes shut and shook his head. "Not at all."

"How do you know what I'm thinking?" Betsy asked.

"Honey, calm down." Mr. Williams reached out and put his hand on his wife's wrist. "Let's give them the benefit of the doubt."

"The benefit of the doubt? My daughter disappears and these two are as thick as thieves. Every time I turn around they're together."

At this proclamation, Natalie rose. She walked right up to Mrs. Williams. "You want to know why I've been talking to Jake? Is that it?" Natalie glared at Meredith's mother. "You think maybe I've been hitting on him, or I have some sort of infatuation with him?"

"Well, don't you?" Mrs. Williams gave her the evil eye. Mr. Williams set his gaze on his coffee cup.

"No. I don't," Natalie said. "And if you really understood what I've been going through, you would know first-hand. The truth is, Mrs. Williams, I already have a boyfriend. Or, rather, I *had* a boyfriend."

Oh boy. The plot really was thickening now. Maybe my

suspicions about Natalie and Jake had been wrong, after all.

Betsy shook her head. "I don't believe you. I've known you for two years, Natalie, and I've never seen you with any other guys than Jake and Kevin."

"Exactly." Natalie gave her a knowing look and crossed her arms at her chest. "You just answered your own question."

Mr. Williams' brow slanted into a frown. "What are you saying?"

Betsy's eyes widened. "Are you trying to tell us that you and Kevin are. . ."

"*Were*," Natalie said, and then sat back down, her lips curling down in a frown. "Not *are*. Kevin and I *were* a couple, but we ended it one week before getting on the ship. I found out that he was just using me to get to one of my friends. He wasn't really interested in me at all."

"So, he broke your heart and now you're seeking comfort from Jake?" Betsy asked. "Is that it?"

"No. There's a lot more to it than that, Mrs. Williams. Jake has been counseling me, that's all. And I had to tell him about Kevin because it affects him personally."

"What did she tell you?" I turned to Kevin.

"Well. . ." He raked his fingers through his hair. "She just told me on the first night of the cruise that Kevin broke her heart. I honestly had no idea until then. On the day we left I thought everything was great, so I thought they were still a couple."

"That's what I wanted everyone to think" Natalie said. "I didn't want my problems to ruin my best friend's wedding, so I thought I could just coast my way through this week and then get back to the business of dealing with the fallout once I got home."

"Fallout? What fallout?" Sheila asked.

At this question, Natalie burst into tears. The whole thing was a repeat of what had happened in the chapel the other night. I reached for a napkin and handed it to her. She used it to dry her eyes then looked at Betsy.

"Do you really want to know what's going on with me, Mrs. Williams? If so, I'll tell you."

"Of course I want to know." Betsy leaned back in her chair, a look of anticipation on her face.

"The truth is. . ." Natalie's voice softened to a whisper. "The truth is, I'm pregnant."

You could've heard a pin drop at that one.

"W-what?" Mrs. Williams asked. "Why didn't you tell us?"

"Because I felt like an idiot. Kevin and I had only been dating a few weeks and I let things go too far, too fast. The whole thing was a huge mistake and now I'm. . .I'm. . ." The sobbing began again. At this point people in nearby booths were looking our way.

Not that it stopped the flow of tears from Natalie. She looked up at us, little hiccups of breath between the cries. "Meredith. Doesn't. Know." She released a slow breath. "*No* one knew until I told Jake the day after Meredith disappeared. That's why you've seen me talking to Jake so much, Mrs. Williams. I wasn't hitting on him. I was just warning him."

"...about my so-called best friend." Jake's expression hardened. "That was my first clue that Kevin had actually done more than break her heart."

"Wait." I put my hand up in the air. "Are you saying that Kevin knows about the baby and broke up with you anyway?"

Natalie nodded and then started crying again. "He. Never. Really. Cared. About. Me!"

Jake took over as Natalie was rocked with sobs. "From what Natalie has told me, Kevin's had a weird infatuation with Meredith."

"He's denied it, but I would catch him flirting with her or looking at pictures of her." Natalie shook her head. "Nothing I can prove. Just a feeling."

"So, you're saying that our fun-loving Kevin is in love with Meredith?" Mrs. Williams shook her head. "Does she know this?"

"I know Meredith better than anyone," Jake said. "And I'm convinced she didn't—er, doesn't—know anything about Kevin's infatuation. Heck, he's my best friend and I didn't even pick up on it, so he's apparently a great actor."

"Apparently," I chimed in.

"I'd give the guy an academy award," Sheila added. "I bought his happy-go-lucky attitude all the way."

"Me too." Mrs. Williams' eyes filled with tears.

"Well, how do you think I feel?" Jake asked. "But ever since Natalie told me, I've been racking my brain to think of things I might've missed. And to make matters worse, I'm rooming with the guy? You know?" He paused. "Well, I was. Until a couple of nights ago. I booted him the minute Natalie told me about his reaction to the baby. The guy is a total jerk."

We all sat in silence for a moment after Natalie's heartbreaking story. After awhile Betsy moved over to sit beside her, and ended up wrapping the young woman in her arms. As she lifted her arm over the young woman's shoulders I couldn't help but feel a wave of relief wash over me. Natalie wasn't responsible. Jake wasn't responsible. And I no longer got the feeling the bride's mother had kidnapped her own daughter.

Really, that only left one suspect.

"Do you think Kevin had something to do with Meredith's disappearance?" I asked after a couple more minutes of thinking it through.

"I thought about that, of course." Jake paused and I could read the pain in his eyes. "But if he really cares about her as much as I suspect, he wouldn't do anything to hurt her. And like I said, he's been with me the whole time. He was on our bus coming back from Cozumel, remember? I've been with the guy non-stop."

"Yes, I remember. So, he wasn't the one responsible. He couldn't be."

"Finally I broke the silence with a question. "Jake, can I ask you something?"

"Sure. Anything."

"Does Meredith have a cell phone?"

"Of course."

"Has anyone checked to see if it's been used?" I asked.

"Used?" He gave me a curious look. "How would we do that?"

"Call the cell provider."

"Maybe that's something the Coast Guard is doing. But, to be honest from the minute they found out she got back onto the ship, they've having been taking this as seriously. They think she's just avoiding me."

"I'm sure she's not. But tell me, what does her cell phone look like?"

"It's a brand new i-Phone."

"In a case?"

He paused and appeared to be thinking. "Yes. It's kind of a teal looking. . ." He paused and shook his head. "No, that's the old phone. The new one is in a pink case, I think."

"Pink with sparkles?"

"Yes, that's right." He nodded. "Why?"

"Well, I'm following a hunch here, but I'd be willing to bet my hunch is right. I paused and allowed my thoughts to swirl. After a moment, Sheila pulled out her camera and started showing off photos of the trip, probably a good idea to distract everyone. Well, until she got to the photo of Kevin climbing Dunn's River Falls.

The moment my gaze fell on that photo the strangest thought hit me. It had nothing to do with Kevin. Not really. But look at the photo stirred up a memory, something that hadn't made any sense in the moment. Right now, however, it made perfect sense.

I pushed my chair back and stood up.

"Annie?" Warren glanced up at me.

"Warren. We have to go back to the security office."

"But we were just there," Sheila said. "It didn't get us anywhere."

"Oh yes it did." I glanced at the group, my thoughts not tumbling. "Folks, I think I know where Meredith is."

"W-what?" Mrs. Williams rose. "Where?"

"Well, I don't know exactly where she is, but I have a strong suspicion. Do you guys want to come with me?"

Apparently they did. All of them. We buzzed through the crowd to the security office. This time the officer greeted me with a groan. "Mrs. Peterson? Here to do my job for me again?"

"No sir," I said. "Just here to confirm a suspicion. Do you mind if I take another look at that photo of the Meredith boarding the ship?"

He shrugged and pulled it up once more. "Whatever you like."

It filled the screen and I felt instantaneous joy as the realization hit. "Look! There's our answer!" I pointed, not at Meredith's picture, but at the woman behind her. "Can you zoom in?"

"Sure." The officer enlarged the photo and I pointed once more. "See? That's what I'm talking about." I pointed at a upper arm of the woman standing in line directly behind Meredith. "Do you recognize that?"

"Not really." Sheila looked perplexed. "Should I?"

"You should. We saw it that day on the top deck when the Calypso band was playing, and again on the night we saw the 50s review. I remember you commented about what it would look like when she got older and developed—"

"Wings." Sheila grinned then held out her upper arms to show the security guy what she meant. "When you get old, your upper arms get flabby." She demonstrated with a back and forth movement. "Fascinating to watch, right?"

The guy cleared his throat.

"You're missing my point, Sheila." I pointed at the tattoo again. There's only one person on this ship who has a tattoo like that and she's directly related to someone in the wedding party, someone who happens to be infatuated with the missing bride."

Natalie gasped. "Oh, Mrs. Peterson!"

"That's it!"

Betsy shook her head. "Wait, you mean Kevin's cousin, Kenzie? You think she had something to do with this?"

"I am. Don't you find it odd that she was standing directly behind Meredith as she boarded the ship and didn't bother mentioning that fact to Jake later on when they were introduced?"

"That's right." Jake paced the office now. "But standing behind her in line at customs doesn't prove she was up to anything. Maybe she didn't even recognize Meredith. You know?"

"I know it's too big a coincidence to ignore. So, who's coming with me?"

"Where are we going?" the security officer asked.

"To find a certain singer to ask a few questions. And if I'm right about her, she's going to be singing a completely different tune."

Without waiting for anyone to join me, I turned on my heels and raced out of the security office, headed straight for the theater.

Chapter Eleven

BLUE OCEAN FLOOR

The days pass happily with me wherever my ship sails.
—Joshua Slocum

The security officer eventually caught up with me and led the way to the theater. "They're in rehearsal right now," he said.

"I know. Perfect timing." I kept pace with him, in spite of the pain coming from my aching thighs. Behind me, the rest of the group followed.

A couple of minutes later we arrived at the locked doors of the Metropolis Theater. The security guard used his key to open the door and then stepped inside. I followed on his heels. He turned to face me and put his hand up. "Let me take it from here, Mrs. Peterson."

"If you don't mind, I really feel like I need to go with you." I didn't intend to plead, but it probably sounded that way. "The others can stay here if you like, but I need to go. I think I can get her to open up. Woman to woman...you know?"

He sighed and led the way. When we got near the stage I saw the performers rehearsing. I could tell Kenzie was there because her voice rang out, crystal clear, as she sang Someone to Watch Over Me. Ironic. The security guard approached the steps leading up to the stage, his pace a lot faster than mine. I tried to keep up but couldn't. This was a man on a mission. We reached center stage and he hollered out for the music to stop.

The director rose from his seat in the front row, clearly agitated. "You know we've only got an hour to rehearse. Why are you interrupting us?"

"We've got an emergency and it involves someone in your cast." The security guard looked as anxious as I felt.

"An emergency?" Several of the cast members talked amongst themselves, but I noticed Kenzie taking a couple of steps back until her body was half-hidden behind another cast member.

"We need to talk to Kenzie." The security guard pointed her out. "And we need to talk now."

"How long will this take? The director looked more annoyed than ever. "She carries this scene."

"Yes, she carries this scene all right." I don't know where the courage to speak those words came from. "And that's why we need to talk to her."

The security officer turned and gave me a warning look. "I'll handle this, Mrs. Peterson."

"Right, right." I clamped my lips shut.

Kenzie, we need you to come with us to answer some questions."

"W-why?" She didn't budge. "I haven't done anything wrong."

"I didn't say you did anything wrong. I said this was an emergency." The officer's brow furrowed. "But your response says a lot."

"More than she knows," I whispered to myself.

Kenzie brushed her hair over her shoulder and shrugged, as if she found all of this to be an annoyance. "Well, I don't have anything to hide."

"Except a bride," I whispered.

"But I need to be back as quick as possible because I'm the lead in tonight's show. Right, Matt?" She looked at the director who nodded.

Several other cast members groaned. One girl even rolled her eyes.

With a confident swagger, Kenzie marched down the steps, up the aisle of the theater, to the foyer.

"What's all this about?" She put her hands on her hips.

"I think you already know." I gave her the evil eye and she flinched

"Nothing could be farther from the truth. I know nothing."

"Let's start with a simple question," I said. "Where is she?"

"Who? Where's who?" Kenzie flipped her hair.

"You know who," the officer said. "Meredith Williams."

"There's no one with that name in our cast and you know perfectly well I don't have time to get to know the passengers."

"This is one passenger you took the time to get to know, thanks to your cousin."

"M-my cousin?" For a moment, her Kenzie's façade seemed to fade. "What do you mean?"

"I mean, we're holding your cousin, Kevin, in a security cell."

Interesting tactic, for the officer to lie like that. Still, I played along.

"W-why?" Kenzie paled.

"You know exactly why," the officer said.

"What did he tell you?" Kenzie began to pace as her anger took over. She turned back to face us, eyes narrowed to slits. "He's such a liar. You can't believe anything he says."

"Actually, he was brutally honest." The officer crossed his arms and leaned against the stair railing, as if completely confident. "Told us the whole story of how the two of you managed to get the bride's attention that day at the beach in Cozumel."

"How you offered her a lift in the cab on your way back," I added. "How you came through security with her, and then somehow manipulated her to follow you."

Okay, so I was guessing at the cab part, but I had a feeling my speculations weren't far off.

"You're crazy." Her expression hardened. "And I want to talk to my attorney."

"With over three thousand passengers on-board, I'm sure we can find you one," I said. "But it's a little pointless, if you want to truth. There's no rule of law out on the open seas." I took a step in Kenzie's direction. "What I want to know is how you got her to go with you to your cabin."

"M-my cabin?" Kenzie flinched.

"Sure. That's where she is, right?" I put m hands on my hips. "And how did you keep her there all this time? Assuming she's still there now, I mean."

Kenzie turned and looked as if she might bolt. The officer took her by the arm and turned her around. Seconds later we heard the click of handcuffs as he arrested her. "You're coming with me, Kenzie."

"No!" The director's voice rang out from the stage. "She's our featured singer at the closing show tonight. We need her."

"Well, we need her more," the officer countered, his pitch elevated.

"And trust me, in a cabin down in the crew's quarters there's a girl who needs all of us even more." I spoke the words, confident they were true.

We all followed on the officer's heels to Kenzie's cabin down on the first deck. Mrs. Williams and Jake whispered back and forth and I could tell they were anxious. Excited. I was too. When we got to the room, Kenzie turned back to glare at me. "If I lose my job over this, I'm going to kill Kevin. This is all his fault."

"I think it's safe to say you've already lost your job," Sheila muttered.

"I didn't need his stupid money, anyway. He. . .he bribed me." She turned the key in the door.

"Bribed you. . .how?" the officer asked.

"Let me answer that." I put my hand up, like in a kid in a classroom. "You aren't really who you say you are. You weren't trained at Julliard. You didn't perform on Broadway. In fact, you didn't even graduate from Junior College. Your biggest claim to fame is playing the role of Juliet in your high school's production of Shakespeare's greatest play."

"Wow, Annie." Sheila gave me an admiring look. "How did you know all of that?"

"Oh, a little super-sleuthing on my part." I grinned. "Actually, I used my $50 onboard credit from the travel agent to buy some Internet access yesterday morning. I did a little research on Kenzie Jamison here." I faced her head-on. "And that brings up another point. Your real name isn't Kenzie Jamison at all, is it?"

"Of course I'm Kenzie Jamison."

"No, you're Mary Sue Johnson from Wichita Falls, not Kenzie Jamison from New York City."

Anger filled her eyes as she spouted, "I *hate* Kevin."

"He's a jerk," I said. "No doubt about it. But that doesn't change anything I said."

"Open the door, Kenzie," the security officer. "Or should I say open the door, Mary Sue."

The angry young woman sighed and stuck her key care in the slot on the door. The lock clicked open. She led the way inside and we all followed closely behind. When the officer turned on the light we saw Meredith curled up in the bed, out like a light.

Jake rushed her way and knelt down, calling her name over and over again but she wouldn't budge.

"Call for the doctor," I cried.

Sheila picked up the room phone and did just that while Jake and Mrs. Williams did their best to wake Meredith.

"You can try all day but she's not budging." Kenzie rolled her eyes. "Not with the stuff Kevin's had me giving her."

"What kind of stuff?" I asked.

She shrugged. "I dunno. He called it a cocktail. She got the first dose that day at the beach. In her fruit punch." Kenzie's eyes narrowed. "Kevin came prepared. We'll just leave it at that. Prescription stuff. All legal." She blew out a breath. "Anything else you want to know?"

"Yeah. I want to know what sort of song the infamous Kenzie Jamison is going to be singing from inside the jail cell as you await your trial and how many of your fans are going to show up for your debut in the courtroom on the day they convict you."

She didn't get a chance to answer. The officer radioed for help and then dragged Kenzie out of the room just as the doctor arrived. He took one look at Meredith and went to work, checking her pulse. After trying some smelling salts, she seemed to revive a bit.

A huge smile lit her face when she saw Jake. "Ooo, Jakie!" She threw her arms around his neck. "Are we married, baby? Is this our honeymoon suite?" She looked around the stark room and rubbed her eyes.

"Not married yet, baby," He leaned down and covered her face in kisses. "Not yet. And this is definitely not our room."

"How come we're not married? Did I oversleep?" She tried to sit up but couldn't seem to manage it. "The wedding is tonight, right? I was just taking a nap. We have so much to do. I need to get up." She tried again and managed to almost sit.

"Only if you're feeling up to it," he said. "But we have a few things to talk about first."

"Oh, Jakie, you *always* like to talk too much." She giggled and then plopped back down on the pillow again, out cold.

"Let's get her to the sick bay," the doctor said. "I'll call for a stretcher."

"I'm going with you." Jake's words came out shaky. No doubt. The poor guy had tears streaming down his face. So did Natalie and Mr. and Mrs. Williams.

The stretcher arrived in short order but I opted not to go to the sick bay with them. I had something else to take care of first, something very important. I had a pretty strong suspicion I knew just where to find a certain best man. . .and he'd better be ready for me when I got there.

"Annie?" Warren took hold of my hand. "I know what you're thinking."

"You do?" I avoided looking into his eyes.

"Yes." He turned my face toward his and looked me in the eye. "You think you can take care of him on your own, but you can't. We've got to involve the officers in this."

I released a breath and then nodded. "Okay, okay. But I know where he is. I feel sure of this." At this point I turned to face Sheila and Orin. "Would you two go back to security and ask for one of the officers to meet me up on the top deck? At the bar."

"You sure?" Sheila asked.

"Yep. It's mid-afternoon. Kevin always seems to hang out at the bar in the middle of the afternoon. I'd be willing to bet money he's there now, kicking back and waiting for the Calypso band to take the stage. Warren and I will distract him. Just get one of the officers to meet us there as quick as you can."

"Aye aye, Cap'n." Sheila saluted me and then rubbed her burnt forehead. "Ow." She and Orin took off.

Warren shook his head and chuckled. "Annie Peterson, how do you do it?"

"Do what?"

"Figure these things out? How did you know to look up Kenzie's background online? And how did you remember about the rose tattoo?"

"I don't know, Warren. Just a God-thing, I guess." I offered a little shrug. "I don't come up with this stuff on my own."

"Clearly." He gave me a little kiss on the forehead. "Sorry if that hurt."

"Actually, I'm not in as much pain anymore." I kissed him squarely on the mouth. "In fact. . .I'm feeling so good that we might just celebrate later, if you know what I mean." I tried to wink but got an eyelash in my eye and ended up fighting to get it out. So much for romance.

Warren laughed and then pulled me into his arms. "I will take you up on that, Annie, but I suspect we're going to have a busy night. If the bride-to-be thinks this is her wedding day, she might actually want to go through with it, as if nothing had happened."

"Maybe." I paused to think it through. "Oh, I think my sunburn is well enough that I can get into my nice dress. It's formal night, anyway, right? And we're going to have our picture taken with the captain on the Promenade deck? And then there's the big parade? Right?"

"Annie, Annie. . ." He put his hand up to stop me. "Slow down. Let's catch the bad guy and then worry about what you're going to wear to formal night. Okay?"

"Okay." I sighed. "Only, I really want to look nice, just in case they go through with the wedding. Do you think my blue silk dress is nice enough? I brought it, but I'm torn. Maybe I'll wear the red. If you don't think red is too brazen, I mean."

He put his hand over my mouth and then laughed. Pulling me close, he placed tender kisses on my cheeks. "C'mon, Agatha Annie. Let's go up to the top deck and find Kevin. The rest? Well, I have a sneaking suspicion it'll take care of itself."

It turned out Warren wasn't kidding when he said the rest would take care of itself. The final night of the cruise ended up being the best night of the cruise. With calm waters the ship sailed on toward Galveston, steady and peaceful. We stood in line to meet the Captain—me in my blue silk dress, and Warren in his finest suit and tie. Sheila wore her hot pink maxi-dress and Orin grumbled when she made him put on a tie with his dress shirt and slacks.

As we stepped into place beside the Captain, he asked our names. The moment I said "Annie Peterson" he reached for my hand and gave it a squeeze. "Well then, Mrs. Peterson, I think we need to get at least one photo of just the two of us, since you single-handedly solved a crime, found a missing bride and saved the day, all while out on the open seas."

"Aw, it was nothing."

"Pretty sure it was something to the bride and groom." He gave me a little wink.

I felt my cheeks grow hot but didn't argue with the man. If the Captain of the *Navigator of the Seas* wanted a picture with me, who was I to complain?

After getting a couple of photos from different angles, Warren joined us. Then we looked on as Sheila and Orin stepped into place next to the Captain. She gave a thumbs up just as the photographer snapped the photo.

"Aw, Annie, that was awesome." Sheila looped her arm through mine and we headed off toward the dining hall with our fellas following behind. "You got your picture taken with the Captain. All by your lonesome! You're going to be the hit of Clarksborough P.A. when everyone finds out Agatha Annie's been at it again."

I stopped walking and shook my head. "Nah. I'd be just fine

Don't Rock the Boat

if no one knew, to be honest. This whole trip. . ." I paused and gazed into her eyes. "It wasn't about crime-solving. It was about spending time with the people I love." I reached for her hand and gave it a squeeze. "You know that, right? You know how much I cherish you? You're my best friend in the world and this week will go down in history as the finest vacation I've ever taken."

"With the finest food." Orin stepped into place beside Sheila and rubbed his belly.

"And the best shows," Sheila added. "Unless you count that one actress who turned out to be such a phony." She rolled her eyes and then laughed.

"True." I nodded and then gave her a hug. "Point is, I'm glad we were able to do this. And I'd do it all over again if you asked."

"Hopefully not too soon," Warren said. "I think I've gained ten pounds."

"Me too, but I don't care. I'll work it off when we get home."

"Home." Sheila repeated the word and nodded. "We're going home tomorrow."

"Mm-hmm," I said. "So let's enjoy our last few hours."

We headed into the dining hall and greeted our waiter with envelopes filled with cash. A wonderful tip for excellent service. Then, just as we took our seats, the whole wedding party appeared. Well, all but the best man, who was, from all we'd been told, a little busy in the jail cell on deck one. The bride seemed alert and happy, a far cry from the way she'd been a few hours prior.

She still appeared to be reeling from all that had happened.

"Are you sure it's Friday?" she asked several times. "I thought we were getting married on Tuesday?"

"We were," Jake said, and then smiled. "But I will marry you on a Friday. Or a Saturday. Or a Sunday. Or any day you say."

"I say today!" She leaned over and gave him a kiss.

"Do you think the chapel is available?" I asked. "I could talk with the Captain. He happens to be a good friend of mine." A little wink followed.

"Actually, the doctor already called the Captain earlier and he stopped by for a visit when we were in the sick bay," Jake said. "He offered something a little nicer than the chapel."

"Nicer?" Sheila and I spoke in unison.

"What do you mean?" I asked.

"I mean. . ." Jake's face lit into the brightest smile. "Tonight's farewell performance in the theater is going to be a little shorter than usual, thanks to a missing actress."

"Ah. I see."

"So, he asked if we wanted to have some very special guests at our ceremony," Jake added. "Say, a couple thousand of them."

Meredith giggled. "The whole audience is invited to stay and watch."

"I wonder if they'll all give you presents?" Sheila asked. "That'd be a lot to haul home."

"Surely not," Jake responded. "But to be honest, I've already got the best gift a man could ever get." He gazed at his bride-to-be, his eyes filled with tears. She leaned over and gave him a kiss so sweet it brought tears to my eyes, too.

Before long the bride's parents appeared, all dressed up. We pulled in extra chairs and asked them to join us. I still couldn't get over the fact that Meredith looked so good. It took a lengthy conversation from Natalie to explain that the medications truly had worn off.

"The doctor assured us she was fine." Natalie spoke quietly, filling me in on the details. "He checked her out and she's going to be all right." Tears flowed. "I don't know what I'd do without her, Annie. She's my best friend."

I glanced across the table at Sheila, who gabbed joyfully with Mrs. Williams. I understood that "best friend" thing better than she knew.

"I know she's gonna stick by you, Natalie." I gazed into the young woman's eyes. "But if you need anything. . .anything at all. . .I want you to call me." I reached inside my purse and came out with a pen, which I used to scribble my phone number on a sugar packet. "Promise you won't forget? You can even come to Pennsylvania and spend time with us, if you want."

"Do you mean that, Mrs. Peterson?"

"I do. I happen to have some daughters not much older than you. One of them is expecting a baby right now." As I spoke those words my heart twisted within me. Suddenly I couldn't wait to get home to see Candy, Brandi, Devin and my sweet pups.

But first. . .well, first I had a wedding to attend. And, if what these fine folks had said was true, it was sure to be a doozie!

Epilogue

DEEPER WATER

There is probably no more obnoxious class of citizen, taken end for end, than the returning vacationist.
—Robert Benchley

The wedding turned out to be the most epic event of the whole week. The Captain pulled out all the stops, giving the happy couple a ceremony they wouldn't soon forget. Meredith looked beautiful in her gorgeous white gown and Jake's tears flowed from the start of the ceremony to the finish.

Best of all? The audience members went crazy with applause when the I Do's were spoken. And sitting front and center, with the parents of the happy couple? Agatha Annie and her crew. Oh, what bliss!

We talked about the wedding all night long, and then again the next day after we disembarked the ship. In fact, we couldn't stop talking about it as we drove from Galveston to Houston to catch our flight home on Sunday afternoon. Only when we climbed aboard the plane for Philly did the chattering come to a halt. By then, we were all wiped out.

When the pilot's voice came on, letting us know we were

about to begin our descent into the Philadelphia area, I could hardly believe it. I must've snoozed my way from Houston to Philly. The whole thing felt like a dream. Just as quickly, my heart was flooded with excitement. I could hardly wait to see my kids. And granddaughter. And puppies.

A text came through from Candy, instructing us to bring Sheila and Orin to our house instead of dropping them off at their place.

"She must be up to something," I said.

"Sounds like it." Warren smiled. "You know how are girls are. . .just like their mama."

"Mm-hmm."

We arrived to find streamers and balloons taped to our front door.

"What do we have here?" Sheila asked, and then yawned.

"Looks like a party." I opened the door and found our living room filled with guests. Brandi, Candy and all of our friends from church. Wow!

"Welcome home!" rang out from the crowd.

Little Maddy came tearing across the room and wrapped her arms around my leg. I kissed her, tears now streaming.

"Nina, Nina!" she said. "I miss you!"

"I miss you too, baby girl," I said, and then swept her into my arms for a final hug.

I'd just started to greet the others when the sound of yipping caught my attention. After putting Maddy down, I knelt to give Sasha and Copper a thousand hugs and kisses. Approximately. "Where were you two when I needed you this week?" I asked. "I had to solve a crime without you. We can't ever let that happen again, you hear me? Oh, you would've loved it! We had the best time ever!"

"Um, Mom?" Candy's voice sounded and I looked up to discover both of my girls standing nearby.

"Well, I like that." Brandi said.

"Yeah, the dogs get all the attention." A very pregnant Candy rolled her eyes. "What are we, chopped liver?"

"Of course not." I rose and gave my girls the biggest hugs ever. "The puppies are just more demanding."

"You can say that again." Candy rolled her eyes. "Don't even ask me how it went with Sasha and Copper while you were gone. I might just tell you."

"Oops." I had a feeling we'd talk about this later. For now, however, I had one thing to do—put the bright blue Caribbean out of my mind, once and for all, and focus on the people right in front of me.

With my hubby carrying on about his pirate ship adventures and my best friend already sharing the news of how I'd solved a crime aboard the *Navigator of the Seas*, I had a feeling that was going to be a little easier said than done.

Don't Miss the Rest of THE BRIDAL MAYHEM MYSTERIES SERIES

THE *Wedding* CAPER

BRIDAL MAYHEM MYSTERIES #1

Join Annie Peterson, mother of the bride, as she solve crimes on her way to the wedding. In book one (The Wedding Caper) a $25,000 night deposit mysteriously disappears from the Clark County Savings and Loan, and Annie Peterson takes on the role of amateur sleuth to solve the mystery. Only one problem. . .she knows nothing about crime solving! With loads of humor and just enough of a mystery to make you wonder whodunit, this story is perfect for a cozy read.

Gone with the *Groom*

Bridal Mayhem Mysteries #2

What's a frenzied mother of the bride to do? The best laid plans of brides and men go awry when Annie Peterson's future son-in-law Scott disappears. Have pre-wedding jitters caused Brandi's fiancé to take flight, or are more sinister forces at work? Surely Annie can solve the riddle. But who could be behind this apparent kidnapping caper? Maybe the drug company Scott works for has hidden motives. Perhaps it's the handiwork of Otis, Scott's deceitful dad. But then again it could be the shady wedding photographer, or the "political enemies" of Scott's mother. Will Annie solve the mystery and recover the missing groom in time for the wedding? Join inspirational author Janice Thompson for another rollicking good time in the second installment of the Bridal Mayhem Mysteries Series.

Pushing up *Daisies*

Bridal Mayhem Mysteries #3

Annie Peterson, mother of the bride, has just married off her oldest daughter but still has another ceremony/reception to plan for Brandi's twin sister, Candy.

When Annie and her daughter visit the Clarksborough, Pennsylvania, florist shop, Flowers by Fiona, to order Gerber daisies for the big day, Annie's dachshund, Sasha, somehow escapes from the car. Sasha ends up in the floral delivery truck with young driver Justin Bastrop, en route to a delivery. Ironically, Justin stumbles into a crime scene at the local funeral home— complete with one too many dead bodies. The funeral director, Eddie Moyer, is D.O.A. and Sasha is missing. Possibly for good.

Who is behind the funeral home murder? Is the local florist, Fiona Sullivan, somehow involved? Or could it be the delivery driver, Justin? After all, he's been angry at Eddie Moyer for years, ever since the old guy fired him while he was in his teens. Then again, there is that matter of the disgruntled family member to consider. Roger Kratz has held a grudge against Eddie Moyer for weeks, feeling he was overcharged for his wife's funeral service. Annie dives into the investigation full steam ahead, hoping to solve the crime. Will she solve this riddle in time for her daughter's ceremony? And, will Sasha arrive home safely?

The *Perfect* Match

BRIDAL MAYHEM MYSTERIES #4

Join Annie Peterson as she follows the clues to discover who set fire to the local dating service, the Perfect Match. Is the arsonist the financially strapped widow who owns the matchmaking business, a mismatched newspaper editor, an unsatisfied and unmarried forty-something customer, or the new female investigator who, except for her suspicious past, seems the ideal mate for Annie's son Devin? The race is on—to see whether or not Annie and her cohorts can solve the crime before another building is burned to the ground and before Devin becomes enamored of the woman who may be Ms. Wrong.

Catering to Disaster

BRIDAL MAYHEM MYSTERIES #5

Join Annie Peterson, mother of the brides as she solves another whodunit! In this light-hearted story, someone has poisoned over a hundred wedding guests. Did the caterer, Annie's friend Janetta, deliberately plan this scheme, or are there more sinister forces at work?

About the Author

Award-winning author Janice Thompson got her start in the industry writing screenplays and musical comedies for the stage. Janice has published over 100 books for the Christian market, crossing genre lines to write cozy mysteries, historicals, romances, nonfiction books, devotionals, children's books and more. She particularly enjoys writing light-hearted, comedic tales because she enjoys making readers laugh. Janice is passionate about her faith and does all she can to share the joy of the Lord with others, which is why she particularly enjoys writing. Her tagline, "Love, Laughter, and Happily Ever Afters!" sums up her take on life.

Janice lives in Spring, Texas, where she leads a rich life with her family, a host of writing friends, and two mischievous dachshunds. When she's not busy writing or playing with her eight grandchildren, she can be found in the kitchen, baking specialty cakes and cookies for friends and loved ones. No matter what Janice is cooking up—books, cakes, cookies or mischief—she does her best to keep the Lord at the center of it all. You can find out more about this wacky author at www.janiceathompson.com. Sign up for Janice's Newsletter for all of her writing-related updates and you'll get a free copy of her Nina's Cakes, Cookies and Candies cookbook!

Made in the USA
San Bernardino, CA
20 September 2018